DISCARDED

the most dangerous thing

D1562565

LEANNE LIEBERMAN

ORCA BOOK PUBLISHERS

Library and Archives Canada Cataloguing in Publication

Lieberman, Leanne, 1974–, author
The most dangerous thing / Leanne Lieberman.

Issued also in print and electronic formats.
ISBN 978-1-4598-1184-3 (paperback).—ISBN 978-1-4598-1185-0 (pdf).—
ISBN 978-1-4598-1186-7 (epub)

I. Title.
PS8623.I36M67.2017   jC813'.6   C2016-904490-4
C2016-904491-2

First published in the United States, 2016
Library of Congress Control Number: 2016950079

Summary: In this novel for teens, Sydney grapples with depression, social anxiety
and her growing desire for a physical relationship with her boyfriend.

*Orca Book Publishers is dedicated to preserving the environment and has
printed this book on Forest Stewardship Council® certified paper.*

Orca Book Publishers gratefully acknowledges the support for its publishing
programs provided by the following agencies: the Government of Canada through the
Canada Book Fund and the Canada Council for the Arts, and the Province of British
Columbia through the BC Arts Council and the Book Publishing Tax Credit.

Cover image by Getty Images and Dreamstime.com.
Hand lettering by Kristi-Lea Abramson.
Design by Jenn Playford
Author photo by Bernard Clark

ORCA BOOK PUBLISHERS
www.orcabook.com

Printed and bound in Canada.

20 19 18 17 • 4 3 2 1

For my sister, Marcy, and my Gibridge sisters.

One

BY SIX THIRTY MY EYES ARE wide open in the dim morning light, but I can't move. There's a weight on my chest holding me down with fierce intensity. I need to roll over, pick up my phone and open the Sudoku app. Today I'm having trouble rolling over for the phone, the weight is so great. This is new. Come on, I tell myself, get going. If I can beat the game, then I can get out of bed. Then I'll be able to do all the other things, like putting my feet on the floor and getting dressed and brushing my teeth. By then, half the battle will be won.

I still haven't picked up my phone. My eyes feel like deadweights, like someone has bolted them into my face. Not even the new pink ballet flats I planned to wear today can lure me out of bed.

I need to get up so I can go to school, graduate and then go to university to study commerce. Then I can get a great job and make enough money to buy a condo I can hide in. I know this isn't the best logic, but it forces me to reach for my phone and open the Sudoku app. If I lose I don't have to get out of bed, but if I win I have to get up.

I always win, and by seven I am in the shower.

Once I get going, I can shake off most of the heavy feeling, blast some of the fog out of my brain. It is almost always there to some degree, weighing me down. At least at school, in classes like math and chem, I can forget about it. There's no room in my brain for the fog when I'm trying to solve a calculus problem.

I bike to school and grind through my morning classes without making too much eye contact, barely saying hi to my lab partner, Paul. By lunch I'm ready to eat my bagel with cream cheese, cucumber and sprouts, my apple and my brownie, and talk to Sofia and Fen.

Sofia is waiting for me by our lockers. She looks me up and down, checking out my outfit: leggings, my favorite blue-and-white-striped, long-sleeve T-shirt, a blue blazer and a pearl necklace.

"What's with the pearls?" she asks.

"They're not real," I say, stroking the shiny beads. "I thought they would be good with my jacket for the investor's club."

"Does that start today?" Sofia looks stricken.

"Yep. You promised."

"Yeah yeah." Sofia opens her locker and pulls out a yogurt. "Fine, let's go meet the junior investors."

"Is Fen coming?" I look around for him.

"No," Sofia says, "he said he was going to work out at lunch today."

Fen has recently become entirely about his body. He even joined the rugby team, although he dislocated his shoulder last term.

Sofia, Fen and I met in eighth grade because we were assigned lockers next to each other. Sofia introduced herself by complimenting me on the sparkly shoelaces in my Converse sneakers. I had worn them because my regular white laces had broken that morning, and the only ones I could find were these gold-and-silver ones my sister, Abby, gave me. Sofia's taller than me, very skinny and really into fashion. Today she has on tall black boots, leggings and this kind of complicated tunic top with pieces of ripped fabric hanging from the shoulders. Even though Sofia also hangs out with other artsy kids who want to study fashion design, we still have our lockers in the same place as we did in eighth grade three years ago.

Sofia and I head down the hall to the math wing, where the investor's club meets. "I think you're going to get into this investing thing. It's all about making money," I say. Sofia and I both believe money can make you happy, or at least happier.

"I do like money," Sofia says. "I just like design and fashion better."

"You need some business sense so you can figure out how to run your fashion house."

"You don't understand," Sofia says, running her fingers through her long hair. "I'm going to be the designer for a company and hire someone like you to figure out the business plan."

"Right," I say. "But you still have to know if my plan is any good."

Sofia sighs. She's willing to come because she knows I can't go by myself, and that's the kind of friend she is.

Sofia and I sit at the back of the room eating our lunch, waiting for Mr. Weston to start. I notice Paul come in with one of his friends and sit close to the door.

Mr. Weston begins by passing out donuts and then starts talking about this year's contest. He pulls up the website on the Smart Board and explains the different kinds of investments we need to make and the timeline of the contest. The team that makes the most money wins a prize. Mr. Weston pulls up a few other sites to help us watch the markets. I follow closely, taking notes on my phone and bookmarking sites. As Mr. Weston speaks, the rest of the fog in my brain dissipates. Not only is the contest about making money, but it's the best kind of applied math—math with risk and strategy.

I whisper to Sofia, "My zeyda will help us. He's been teaching me already, and he's vicious at this kind of stuff."

Sofia nods as if to say, *yeah, yeah, yeah.*

When the first bell rings to signal the end of lunch, we file out of Mr. Weston's room into the hall. Sofia and

THE MOST DANGEROUS THING

I are heading toward our lockers when I hear Paul call, "Hey, Syd." We wait for him to push his way through the crowded hallway.

"I didn't know you were interested in investing," he says.

I nod, forcing myself to look at Paul. We never talk outside of class.

Sofia says, "She does it for real too."

I kick her. "Not really."

Paul grins. "Now I know who to go to for stock tips."

If we stand around talking too long, we'll be late for our afternoon class, so Sofia says, "Gotta go, see you" for both of us.

"Bye," I add.

"Hey, Syd," Paul says. "Do you want to meet after school to work on chem?"

"Um, I'm busy today," I say. I always visit my zeyda on Mondays.

"Can I text you?" Paul asks.

"Sure." Paul and I have texted before about school-work. I give a half wave, and Sofia and I start heading down the hall.

"Do you think he likes you?" Sofia asks.

"Who, Paul? No, he's just my lab partner."

"Maybe, but he was looking at you. I mean, really *looking* at you."

"I didn't notice." This is a lie. I'm also wondering why Paul needs to text me. We could talk in class tomorrow.

"Syd," Sofia says, "that's because you weren't even making eye contact."

"That's not one of my strengths. You know that."

"Well, I think he's into you," Sofia says. "And I think he's kinda cute."

I raise my eyebrows at Sofia. "Yeah, I don't think so."

Sofia lifts her hands in defeat, and I turn away to head down the stairs to my next class. On the way there my phone pings. I stop to look at a message from Paul: **Talk to you later.** I'm not sure what to do with this, so I shove my phone in my pocket and keep on walking.

I've known Paul since eighth grade. We sat next to each other in science class, in the back row, and ended up being lab partners because neither of us knew anyone else in the class. Paul didn't even say hi to me the whole first year. At first I thought it was because he was shy, but then I realized he didn't speak English very well. He would use his translator to figure out the lab sheet, and we would work silently together. He was even worse at making eye contact than I was. Mostly he talked in Cantonese to the kid next to him. I found this a little annoying, but I was used to it. Almost half the kids at my school speak Cantonese or Mandarin at home instead of English. Paul and I were lab partners for ninth-grade science too, but it wasn't until tenth-grade science that he actually started talking to me. I guess he was one of those people who wouldn't speak English out loud until he felt confident. Now he doesn't even have an accent anymore.

This year we're taking chemistry together, and Paul happens to be in my math class too. Sometimes at lunch he'll wander down the hall to my locker and we'll compare our math or finish a lab.

I can also talk to Paul normally, which sounds a little weird, but I have a hard time talking to most people. Paul is easy to be with because he's so relaxed and has such an easy smile. I even told him a math joke once. I called our math class LCD. He didn't get it. I had to explain. LCD, lowest common denominator—get it? It means our class is full of kids who are bad at math, who should be in applied, not academic.

Paul had stared at me. I can't believe you just made a math joke.

I can't believe you didn't get it.

It was a math joke. He looked incredulous.

I continue down the hall to my creative writing class. No one knows I'm taking this elective. Sofia thinks I'm taking English, although if she thought about it, she would realize I took English last term. Eventually my parents will see the course listed on my transcript, but they probably won't pay much attention to it. They don't look closely at my reports because they know I always get high grades, and because Abby's reports are so wildly unpredictable. She'll decide that geometry is interesting and do well, then decide calculus is useless. Or she'll claim the basketball unit in her mandatory gym class is discriminatory because she's under five foot five and refuse to participate.

My writing class is just a class to take for fun. Mostly I'm interested in math, because it's the main prerequisite for commerce and because there's always a correct outcome. Sure, there might be multiple ways to get to the answer, but in the end there's a final resolution. It's not like other subjects, or even life, where there are gray areas and lots of possible answers. When I finish a math test, I go over the answers and then I try to figure out my mark. Sometimes I'll even write it at the top of my test with a question mark. Then I figure out the percentage.

Mom would be very excited if she knew I was taking writing. She's suggested I take something artsy for years. *To expand your horizons*, she says. She likes that I have a plan for financial success, but sometimes she looks at me wistfully and says, *What about a dream, something improbable, a little romantic? Your life shouldn't be too planned out, Syd. Leave some room for spontaneity and art.* Then she'll sigh and say, *When I was your age I wanted to be an actress.* If she's feeling really dramatic, she'll add, *Even your father has artistic dreams.* She means my dad's obsession with architecture. Dad has a collection of books on architectural wonders of the world, everything from the pyramids in Giza to the Burj Al Arab hotel in Dubai. Dad does not have "artistic dreams." He's a civil engineer, and his interest in architecture focuses on the technology and design of structures, mainly bridges. If you have lots of time, he'll lecture you on the beauty of I.M. Pei's Louvre pyramid or Gaudi's La Sagrada Familia.

I take a seat at the back of the writing class. I don't know anyone well in the class, and that's fine with me. So far, the writing assignments have been within my comfort zone. I've even been able to participate in the editing sessions, where you have to read your work out loud to a partner. This guy Dean and I usually work together. He's skinny and wears his hair in a long ponytail, and I can tell he's even more nervous than me. He likes to write sci-fi stuff, the more battle scenes, the better.

In class we've been practicing things like setting a scene and writing dialogue, and there hasn't been too much discussion of art. To me, art is scary. Art is where the dark edges of your life show through. I don't want people to see the fog or the dark inside me.

Sometimes I worry that the fog is showing anyway, that I'm breathing it out everywhere I go. I wish I could put on a fake sunny facade, and people would buy this as my true self, or at least as the self I'm presenting to the world. For the writing class, there's a poetry assignment coming up and a story we'll have to write by the end of the term, but I'm pacing myself. Mrs. Lee, the writing teacher, says stories and poems don't have to be about ourselves. I'm planning on being very creative and very impersonal.

Today we're working on descriptions of people, and that still feels safe. I write a vivid portrait of Abby, starting out with some wordplay. That's mostly what I like to do, breaking down words and then building them up again.

Abigail, a gale, a storm, Abby blowing in and then out, a whirlwind, a whirling wind, a winding whirl, like an unfurling curl, a raging girl.

Abby, a bee, a buzzing bee, so busy, here and there, everywhere, raging, mother hive, alive, a buzzing bee, Abby.

When I have to turn to Dean and share some of my work, I manage to read a whole paragraph out loud to him. My face burns with embarrassment, and I can't look at him. When it's over, I hear him mumble, "I like that," and then my face goes red from the compliment.

After writing class, I have Mandarin. It's a good way to end the day because there's a lot of memorization and "repeat after me" as Mr. Wu, our teacher, tries to get us to say words with the right intonation. I'm not very good at pronouncing the different sounds, but I thought learning Mandarin would be helpful for my business future.

After class I head back down the stairs to my locker. Before I even get there, my phone buzzes. Paul has texted me a picture of a fluffy high-in-the-sky cloud. It's a beautiful picture, but I'm not sure what to do with it. I stare at my screen. Finally I write back, **Nimbostratus?**

Cumulus. Looks like?

Oh, this is a game. Okay. I squint at the picture. **A kitten?**

Maybe. I think a sheep.

I type a smiley face back because I'm not sure what else to write.

As I put my phone down to pack my bag, Paul sends another picture, this one of a cloudy sky with a hole in the center.

? I type back.

It's a fallstreak hole, altocumulus.

This is a little weird. I write back, **You taking grade 9 science again?**

No.

I've got my jacket and backpack on and am strapping on my helmet. **Your turn**, Paul writes.

For what?

Send me a picture.

A cloud?

Anything.

I look out the window. The sky is gray, threatening rain.

Let me think about it.

Fen comes down the hall with his distinctive jerky walk, and I quickly hide my phone, as if he might see the texts from Paul. Fen would want to know all about the texts, ask too many questions and have opinions about them too.

Sometimes I wonder why Sofia and I still hang out with Fen, or why we ever hung out with him in the first place. He's not interested in fashion or finance or even personal grooming beyond the bare necessities of hygiene.

Fenny's also not much to look at. He's very thin and has an awkward Adam's apple, bad acne and a twitchiness about him that makes it hard for him to sit still. Sometimes I feel like suggesting he needs to change his ADHD meds, but that probably wouldn't go over well. Still, he's incredibly smart and patient. He's tutored Sofia in math since eighth grade and proofreads essays for both of us.

Also, Fen got me into long-distance biking. Before I met him, I just rode around the city, more for transportation than sport. Then Fen took me out riding near his grandparents' house out of the city, where there's not much traffic and only countryside to look at, and I've been hooked ever since. Once when we were out there, Fen suggested that maybe we could be more than friends, which was embarrassing and awkward and horrible, and I stammered something that meant no. To Fen's credit, he's never said a word about it again, and he still takes me biking. Still, when I see Fen I think, *Fenny, penny, scrawny neck, chicken neck, lame duck, walks like a duck.*

"How was rugby?" I ask him.

"Grueling." Fen fiddles with his lock.

I step away. "Smells like it."

Fen grins. "One must suffer to look good." He steps away and flexes.

I sigh. "Yeah, Fen, you're way more buff than you used to be."

"Yes!" Fen punches an arm into the air. "I'm at my dad's this weekend. You in for biking?"

"Sure. When?"

"Don't know yet." Fen grins. "Think you'll make the whole ride this time?"

I roll my eyes. "That was just that one time." On our last ride, Fen and his dad had to come find me in the car because I bonked out on the ride back.

Fen's got his backpack and jacket on now and is ready to head outside. "You coming?" he asks.

"What about Sofia?"

"Ah, she's flirting with the new math teacher again. I saw her on my way out."

I shrug and start walking beside Fen. Maybe I'll keep Paul's texts to myself for a while. I'm not sure what to make of them yet anyway. Who sends cloud pictures?

Fen and I head outside into the gray day. It's not raining, but the air is so damp it feels like it is. We get on our bikes and say goodbye. Fen's going to his dad's house, and I'm heading west across the city to Zeyda's house.

Traffic moves slowly, leaving me lots of time to think. Why is Paul sending me pictures? Sofia would say it's because he likes me. She'd ask me if I like him, if maybe I might be in love, and then she'd tell me some long-winded story about her aunt in Croatia who fell in love and what happened to her. It would be one of Sofia's stories that comes to a weird ending with no real conclusion. I've never thought of Paul as a potential boyfriend. I've never thought of anyone that way. Most girls seem to want a boyfriend the way they want a designer purse or a really expensive pair of leather boots—as a status symbol.

Back when we first met, Paul was shorter than me, barely over five feet, and he had a little kid's voice. Now he's at least six inches taller than me and, well, he's a guy. He wears his hair differently too. It used to flop into his eyes. Now it's shorter, and he gels up the front. I pause for a red light and reach for my phone to take a picture of the taillights reflecting in a puddle. I could send that to Paul, call it *my ride*, but maybe that's not the right thing.

I forget about Paul as I get closer to the ocean, closer to Zeyda's neighborhood. He lives on the west side of the city, past Kitsilano, on the way to the university. From the road his house doesn't look like much, just a front door level with the sidewalk and a garage, but the back of the house descends a cliff to the beach, with four different levels and the most amazing views of the ocean, the mountains and downtown. Zeyda and Bubbie built the house in the seventies, and it has a distinctive west-coast style—all cedar and glass—that hasn't been updated in years. My bubbie had a thing for Chinese antiques, and the house is stuffed with vases, ornate tables and scrolls. On clear days you can sit in almost any room and watch the boats go by—sailboats, motorboats, cruise ships and giant container ships going to and from China.

Zeyda has lived alone in the house ever since Bubbie died three years ago. Mom and Dad have been trying to convince him to move to a retirement home because he had a stroke last year, but he refuses. Zeyda can talk and walk again, but he doesn't move very fast and he can't climb stairs, so he lives on the main floor of his house and his caregiver, Crystal, comes every weekday. Zeyda is the most stubborn, opinionated person I know. He's also racist, sexist, grumpy, rude to strangers and cheap. He regularly fights with Mom and threatens to write her out of his will. Still, I visit him all the time. I know he's lonely, and it's my job to help him. Also, I love him.

Zeyda and Bubbie spent a lot of time taking care of Abby and me when we were little, especially me. When I was seven, I fell down the stairs in our house and broke my leg. I was in a cast for a long time. I remember lying on a mattress in the living room, first in a lot of pain and then in total boredom. Mom took some time off work, and Bubbie and Zeyda looked after me the rest of the time. Zeyda spent hours lying on the floor with me, designing winter wear for my paper dolls and teaching me how to play every card game he knew. He also tutored me in my schoolwork, especially math. Bubbie cooked and read to me and told me stories and taught me Yiddish songs. We spent a lot of time looking at her collection of fashion and home-decorating magazines.

Zeyda used to own a coat factory, but ever since he sold it and retired, he spends most of his time managing his money. He's teaching me about investing, and in exchange I'm giving him lessons on how to use a computer so he can do online trading. I've also been showing him how to use social media, but he's not interested in people, only money. Zeyda gave me five thousand dollars for us to invest together. Then he decided we needed to invest another five thousand in Abby's name. It wouldn't be fair to your sister, Zeyda had said, even if she doesn't come and visit.

I didn't bother telling him Abby would visit if he stopped saying sexist things in her presence.

I wheel my bike past the side gate at Zeyda's house and lock it to the fence. The ocean is gray, the tide right in against the base of the house. I take a quick picture of the rocks against the cliff with the ocean coming in. It's not bad, better than the one with the puddle and taillights. I hesitate a moment and then send it to Paul. I'm not sure what it means, but it's a good picture, and if clouds are Paul's thing, then the ocean is mine.

When I was in seventh grade and my anxiety first became really bad, I thought being near the ocean might save me. I thought that if I walked on the beach every day, I could fight off the nervousness I constantly felt. The waves would carry away my unease and leave me with some other feeling, something fresh and new. I biked to the beach almost every day, and if the tide was low I ran as fast as I could on the hard wet sand, until I was breathless, watching the seagulls take flight in front of me.

Sometimes running helped, sometimes it didn't. Still, I carried the idea around in my head for a long time, like a chant. *The ocean will save me.* Sometimes I imagined walking into the water and letting it swallow me up. Not to drown, just to feel the water instead of fear surrounding me. I wasn't crazy though—the ocean is freezing here, except maybe on the hottest summer days. Now I think riding my bike might save me.

I come back to the front of the house and ring the bell. Crystal answers the door. She's barely five feet tall and wears jeans and a sweatshirt, with her hair in a long braid. She has the biggest smile of anyone I've ever met. Even when she's complaining about her kids or worrying about money, she's laughing. I always thought she was about twenty-five until I saw pictures of her kids, who are in their twenties.

"Hi, Sydney," Crystal says. "Your grandfather is waiting for you."

I take off my shoes and jacket and leave my backpack in the front hall. Zeyda's in his usual spot, slumped in his recliner, looking out at the sea. He turns to look at me. "You're late," he says, not smiling.

I kiss the top of his bald head. "I said I'd be here around four."

"If you say 4:00 PM, you should be here at 4:00 PM."

"There was traffic, and I didn't want to get killed on my bike. Besides, you had somewhere to go?"

Zeyda doesn't leave the house much anymore, except to go to his *shul* on Saturdays and occasionally to the casino, if Crystal will take him. She's under pretty strict orders from Mom not to take him too often.

Crystal brings me a mug of mint tea and a cookie like the ones Bubbie used to make, and I sit next to Zeyda by the big window overlooking the sea. "See any whales today?" I ask.

Zeyda shakes his head.

My phone beeps, and I take it out of my pocket. **Nice photo**, Paul writes. **Where?**

I write back, **Near Jericho beach.**

Send another?

Zeyda sits up in his chair and rubs the bags under his eyes. "Who is sending you messages? Your mother?"

"Just a friend."

"Your Sofia?"

"No, a different friend."

"A boyfriend?"

"Not a boyfriend. He sends me pictures of clouds." I hold up the phone to show Zeyda the fallstreak hole.

"What kind of boy sends you things on a phone?"

I'm not sure how to answer that. "A nice one?"

"You like this guy?"

I shrug.

"Is he Jewish?"

"Who cares?" I type, **Maybe later, kinda busy now.**

Okay, see you tomorrow.

"I care," Zeyda says. "It used to be important who you dated, who you married. Now"—he lifts up his hands—"it's nothing."

I try not to roll my eyes when Zeyda says, "That's not how we did it in my day." And then he's quiet, and I know he's thinking about the past again, about Bubbie and his life before his stroke. He used to be more interested in the world around him. Now he doesn't want to go anywhere.

I take a breath. I'm supposed to be cheering him up.

"Did you check the stock prices yet?" I say, pulling out my tablet.

Zeyda's eyes clear. He nods. "The TSX is up, but my oil stocks are down. It's those environmentalists protesting again!"

I cut Zeyda off before he gets going on politics and tell him about investor's club and the contest. He looks through my stock options and makes some suggestions, mostly about investing in mining and gold. Apparently natural resources and high tech are what it's all about. At least talking keeps Zeyda in the present and not lost in missing Bubbie and thinking about the way his life used to be. I need to keep him cheered up so I don't get dragged down with him. Zeyda's cloud is even heavier than mine today, and if I'm not careful we'll both be falling into the same dark place, and who will get us out then?

Two

I RIDE HOME ALONG THE WATERFRONT, taking the bike path past Kits Beach and then over to Vanier Point. It's late afternoon, and there aren't too many pedestrians, so I continue through Granville Island and then over to Olympic Village. It's slower than riding the main streets but prettier, although it's raining now. The roads shimmer in the streetlights. Once I get to Main Street there's no choice but the steady uphill slog home.

Mom and Dad both work late on Monday nights, and Abby and I are in charge of making dinner. Usually that means we eat something like tacos or defrost something from the freezer. I hang up my jacket and bike helmet and toss my backpack by the back door. There's something that looks like lasagna defrosting on the counter, so I guess that's what Abby's chosen.

Our house is a small bungalow on what used to be the not-so-fancy side of the city. Now our neighborhood is trendy and expensive. On the main level of our house there's a living room, kitchen, dining room and office. My parents' bedroom is in the attic, up this crazy-steep set of stairs, and Abby and I have bedrooms in the basement and our own rec room with a TV and beanbag chairs. A few years ago Abby and I created a tent in the rec room by hanging fabric from the ceiling. It's big enough for both of us to lie down on cushions. Abby also strung up some Tibetan prayer flags she found in a shop on Main Street and fairy lights. If you turn out all the lights in the room except for the fairy lights, you can pretend you're in a tent in the desert. Most days when I come home, this is where Abby is, curled up with a book or her phone.

I peel back the fabric and crawl onto the cushions. Abby sits up and pulls out her earbuds. "Hey," she says, "where you been?" She smooths her flouncy orange-and-pink skirt over her leggings.

"Visiting Zeyda."

Abby scowls. "Really? How can you spend so much time with him?"

I shrug. Abby and I have had this conversation before.

"Rose and thorn," Abby says. She stretches out her arms expectantly.

I lean back against some cushions. Still sweaty from my bike ride, I peel off the long-sleeve biking shirt I wore riding home. I consider telling her about Paul, but Abby will pounce on this and devour it, and I'm still mulling it over, so I say, "The TSX is up fifty points and I had a great bike ride, so that's my rose. And the thorn, well, Zeyda wasn't in the greatest mood."

Abby says, "Figures," but I can tell she's more interested in telling me her good news, her rose, than listening to my day. "The best part of my day," she announces, "is that I came up with a fantastic idea for the senior drama festival."

I try to look interested. "Which is?"

"I'm going to put on *The Vagina Monologues*." Abby claps her hands, waiting for my reaction.

The Vagina Monologues isn't a play with characters and a plot. It's exactly what it sounds like—a series of monologues about vaginas. Mom took us to see it last year at the university on Valentine's Day. Parts of it were sad and parts of it were funny, but mostly it was embarrassing to listen to women talk about their private parts, especially sitting next to Mom. I'm not sure what Abby thinks I'm going to say, but all I can manage is "Ew" and then "Really?"

Abby doesn't care that I'm grossed out. She's too excited by her own audacity. "It's going to be amazing."

I clutch my phone to my chest. "You want to talk about girl parts at school?"

"Yes. I think it's so important."

"I can't imagine Mr. Edwards is going to approve that," I say.

"He already did."

"He did?"

"Yep. Okay, it's pending administrative approval, but Mr. Edwards said sure."

"Has he read the script?"

"Parts of it. And I already have five other girls who want to be in it."

I shake my head. "And you think I'll come see the play?"

"Yes!" Abby grabs my hand. "Of course you will."

"But you'll be performing something so embarrassing." I shudder and pull my hand back. It was bad enough to sit through the play once, but having to watch Abby perform it will be worse. And Dad will probably want to come. I shudder again. Maybe I'll change schools or get a new last name so no one knows we're related.

"Syd!" Abby gets up on her knees. "This is important. It's not just theater—it's about women's bodies. There are women all over the world who are not in control of their bodies, especially their vaginas. There are women who are denied birth control, and women who are mutilated. Plus, there are all kinds of women and girls who don't know how wonderful—"

"I get it." I cut Abby off before she says something really gross. "Are you going to tell Mom and Dad about the play?"

"Sure. Why not?"

I stare at her until she throws a pillow at me. "Stop that," she says. "You know it freaks me out."

I can't help staring at Abby. It's like she's from another planet. Not only do we not look alike—Abby is very petite, with a curvy body and super-curly blond hair, whereas I'm taller, with straight brownish hair and angles instead of curves—but we are also totally different people. It's not just that I'm shy and she's not. She doesn't seem to feel shame, and I find this weird. Last week Abby was babysitting down the street, and she accidentally locked herself and the kids out of the house. Colby, who is only five, remembered that one of the neighbors had a key to the house, but he couldn't remember which neighbor. So Abby dragged Colby and Morgan, who is only two, up and down the block until they found the right house. Abby cheerfully told me all about it when she got home. I tried to imagine what I would have done. Probably the same thing, but I would have died of embarrassment as I knocked on each door. I'd probably never be able to babysit Colby and Morgan again.

"At least there won't be dancing in the play."

"Says who?" Abby stands up and puts her hands on her hips. "Maybe I'll create a dance of the vaginas just for you." Abby starts to sway her hips and tap her foot. "If my vagina were a dance, what would it be?" she announces to an imaginary audience. She lifts her hands above her head and starts to clap as if she is doing some folk dance. Then she unties the scarf from her hair and starts waving it around. "I know it would definitely be a striptease, perhaps

24

the dance of seven veils." She swings her hips back and forth, the scarf still above her head. "And you, Miss Sydney Mizner? What kind of dance would your vagina do?"

I stuff my head under a cushion while Abby dances herself out of the tent.

Sometimes I think I need to start a support group for introverted people with extroverted siblings.

My vagina does not dance. And neither does the rest of my body. While Abby has spent years in programs with dubious (and mortifying) names like "Gotta Sing! Gotta Dance!" I have spent my time on my bike or with Zeyda or running on the beach. Personally, I don't need to talk about bodies, especially vaginas. A vagina hides because it's private. It does private and sometimes disgusting things to do with sex and babies and periods. And the word *vagina*—it doesn't even rhyme or break down into any parts. It only rhymes with *angina*, which is something to do with your heart not working, and *Regina*, which is a place that should be renamed because saying it makes me blush. Luckily I don't know anyone from there.

The sex ed we get at school hasn't convinced me that vaginas are happy places either. Every year, gym class is interrupted without warning, and instead of volleyball or gymnastics we get shuffled into a classroom to watch doom-and-gloom videos about vaginas and sex. Last year it began with a film on pregnant teens, saddled with babies who sucked up their time and made them poor and unpopular. Then there was a movie on STIs, all the infections you can get from having sex, complete with gross pictures of diseased parts. Basically, it was an hour of oozing sores and miserable-looking girls who wished they'd used a condom before they slept with that guy. The video culminated with a girl who had contracted HIV and might die before her sixteenth birthday.

In the class on birth control, we learned about a bewildering array of pills, injections, patches and weird things to insert in places I don't like to think about, all to avoid pregnancy and all with varying side effects, like weight gain and hair loss. Again we were reminded of the teenage mothers who hadn't protected themselves. The icing on the cake was a film on protecting yourself from harmful relationships. The film focused on girls who were manipulated, stalked, coerced and even beaten by their boyfriends.

By the end of the week I couldn't figure out why anyone would want to have sex, or even a boyfriend or girlfriend. Anything involving a vagina was possibly connected with disease and danger. Since I didn't even talk to boys, I was happy to forget about anything sexual. I believed the sex-ed videos: sex was for adults who could deal with adult problems.

Mom and Dad both come home around eight, and then we eat lasagna with salad and some garlic bread

Dad picked up on his way home. I love lasagna, but I don't have much appetite tonight. Mom tries to ignore her buzzing phone while we eat. She had some important meeting of the hospital executive tonight, and now everyone's weighing in with their opinions. She finally puts it on silent. After dinner Abby excuses herself to go downstairs, Dad drifts to his office to read, and I do some math homework in front of the TV. Mom's trying to relax by watching some cop series that I can't imagine she's interested in, but her phone is back on and she keeps taking calls and returning emails and asking me what she's missing. Finally she turns her phone off and shoves it in her purse. Then she pours herself a glass of wine. "I give up," she says.

"On what?" I ask.

"This day. I'm not answering any more work emails until tomorrow."

I look at the time on my phone. "Tomorrow's only a few hours away."

"Workwise it's more than twelve." Mom runs her fingers through her hair. "Do you think I need a haircut?"

"It's hard to tell." Mom has long curly hair, the kind of curls you can uncoil down past her shoulders and then release and watch them bounce up.

"You okay?" Mom asks. "You didn't eat much at dinner."

"I had a big snack at Zeyda's," I lie.

Mom eyes me critically, and I sit up on the couch and try to look perky. "You look tired," she says.

I am tired, even though I've been sleeping a lot. The fog makes me feel as if I'm carrying a heavy blanket on my back. I try to smile. "No, I'm good."

The fog is top secret, especially from Mom. If anyone knew about it, they'd pay more attention to me, and that would make me feel worse. I tried to look up my symptoms online, and they don't fit into any real category. It's true I'm tired and not that hungry, but I can still concentrate on schoolwork. In fact, concentrating makes me feel better—I can forget the fog for a few minutes. I'm not like those people who feel the whole world is black. The fog is just the latest version of my anxiety, and I'm coping just fine.

If Mom knew about the fog, she'd want to talk about it, even tell other people about it, and that would be unbearable. She'd make me see Dr. Sandhu, our family doctor, or, worse, Dr. Spenser, the therapist I used to see. I've managed not to see her for almost three years by telling everyone that I'm feeling great.

Mom made me see Dr. Spenser the first time at the end of seventh grade. She got suspicious that I wasn't coping well when I started asking if I could be home-schooled or take online courses instead of going to high school. I'd always been a quiet kid, and my small elementary school suited me. When I thought about going to high school, I couldn't imagine being with all those older kids, or making presentations in class. I started reciting multiplication tables to calm myself down, but then I couldn't stop reciting them, and I couldn't sleep.

I was expecting Dr. Spenser to be this old guy with glasses and a tweed jacket. I thought maybe he'd have a couch in his office for patients to lie down on while they talked about themselves, but Dr. Spenser is actually a woman with short, spiky blond hair and funky red-metal glasses. Also, there's no couch in her office, just regular chairs.

Dr. Spenser helped me learn some coping strategies (other than multiplication) to deal with my anxiety. We did a lot of visualization practice together, imagining me going to high school, walking down the hallway, sitting in class, finding my locker, even putting my hand up in class. I still use some of these strategies, although avoiding people is always my first tactic.

Dr. Spenser once asked me what would happen if people were looking at me and listening to me when I put my hand up in class or had to make an oral presentation.

"I might get broken," I told her.

"Then what would happen?" she asked.

I thought about this for a long while before answering. "If I felt broken, it would be even harder to talk to people, and I'd want to stay at home even more." I couldn't explain it any other way.

I'm about to leave the living room when Mom announces, "I think I'll start planning for Passover."

"Isn't that a month away?" Passover is the Jewish holiday that celebrates the Jewish release from slavery in Egypt way back in biblical times. For eight days you're not supposed to eat bread or baked goods that have yeast in them or have risen. Instead you eat *matzah*, which is like a very dry cracker. It tastes good the first day, but by the fourth day it's unbearably dry and bland—plus it's totally constipating. You celebrate the first two nights of Passover with a Seder, which is a dinner with lots of rituals and prayers.

"Yes, only a month away!" Mom yawns and grabs a to-do list from the coffee table.

"It's a little early to start cooking and cleaning." I tidy a stack of mail and magazines. When I find a copy of the Jewish Community Center catalog, I absently flip through the pages.

"I'm not planning that part. I mean the actual Seder."

"What's to plan?" Usually we go to Zeyda's house, and he drones through the readings in this old yellow *Haggadah*, which is a type of prayer book. The Seder goes on forever, and then we eat Crystal's matzah balls. In the JCC catalog I notice a seniors' drop-in group that meets once a week. That's what Zeyda needs— some company. They even have dancing and cards, just

Zeyda's thing. Well, the cards anyway. I fold over the corner of the page.

"This year it's going to be different," Mom says.

"Really?" I look up from the catalog.

"Yep. It's going to be here."

I smirk. "Zeyda is going to love that."

"The torch is being passed. And it's going to be a totally different Seder. I'm going to invite Miri and Todd and the Levs and some other women from my spirituality group."

"Oh," I say. "What about Uncle Mark and Auntie Karen?"

"Yes, them too."

"That sounds crowded." I bet Mom's Seder will be even longer than Zeyda's. "I could be your kitchen help," I suggest, hoping to get out of participating.

"Don't be silly. I already asked Crystal to help out, and besides, I want you to be part of the Seder."

Great. It'll be long and touchy-feely, with lots of extra bits to include oppressed people from around the world. "Do I have to be part of any bibliodrama?" I ask.

Mom clasps her hands together. "What a good idea! You could organize the Levs' kids to act out the story. You could even dramatize the plagues."

"That sounds more like Abby's thing."

"Right. Right." Mom has knotted her hair on top of her head and stuck a pencil through it to keep it off her face, and she's scribbling furiously on her pad. "Do you

think we could get Zeyda to sing 'Go Down, Moses'?
He has such a great baritone."

"You're not serious," I say.

"I guess not. Maybe Dad will do it."

"You're still not serious."

Mom chews on the end of her pen.

"When are you going to tell Zeyda about your new-age intentions?" I ask.

"Not new-age. They're...meaningful. It's Judaism with intent." Mom taps the pen on her knee. "I thought maybe you could tell him next time you're there."

I groan. I'm always the go-between because Zeyda has a soft spot for me. Anytime Mom and Dad have something planned, I'm the one who breaks the news. The biggest deal was Crystal. When Zeyda couldn't live on his own anymore and refused to leave his house, I had to tell Zeyda that Crystal was my friend and that she was coming over for tea with me. The next time Crystal and I came over, this time for dinner, we told him Crystal was a super cook, specializing in Jewish cooking. Zeyda was rightly skeptical, since Crystal is from the Philippines, but she had worked for another Jewish family, so she could make some Jewish specialties, and Mom asked her to make Zeyda's favorite *kouffle* cookies. Zeyda really liked the cookies, and he got used to having her around.

"I think you should share your own bad news," I tell Mom.

Mom sighs. "Zeyda wasn't always this grumpy. He used to play cards with his buddies and tell dirty jokes and tease Uncle Mark and me."

"I remember that from when I was little."

"Good," Mom says. "I hope you'll keep those memories of him."

I nod. Then I head downstairs to my room to get ready for bed. I check my phone one more time before I close my eyes. Fen has sent me a biking article, and Sofia, a link to a shoe site. I look at my stocks for the contest and then check for another text from Paul, but there's just his final **See you tomorrow** after my picture.

Three

THE NEXT MORNING I CAN SENSE the fog before I'm fully awake. I feel it in my fingertips and toes, like weights on the ends of my limbs, pinning me to my bed. The clock blinks 6:30 AM, which means I have half an hour to wrestle my way out of bed, to fight my way out of the heavy darkness. I'd like to roll out from under it, to imagine myself as thin as a piece of paper and leave it hovering in my room while I slink underneath it. Or if I were as light as a cloud, maybe I could rise above it. But as hard as I try and concentrate, neither image works. I grab my phone and play a game of Sudoku instead. It doesn't make me feel any better. Finally I envision seeing Paul at school, and the nervous hum that radiates through me is enough to make me roll out of bed and crawl across the carpet to my closet.

I pause there for a minute, trying to figure out what to wear. Then I see the spot under my clothes that I've left bare, a space big enough to curl up with my knees pulled to my chin. For a moment I want to step into the closet, close the door and forget about school. I quickly grab a pair of jeans and a gray V-neck sweater instead. If I start sitting in the closet, I'll never get going.

I arrive at school just as the first bell rings and slide into a seat next to Paul in chem class. We say hi and then both look away shyly, as if we had never texted. Class starts soon after, and the teacher lectures and we listen, and that's the end of that. I feel the fog settle on me a little more heavily, and it hangs around me as I trudge through the rest of the day.

The same thing happens Wednesday morning, until we start a new lab halfway through the period. Then Paul and I have to talk to each other, at least about the assignment. We don't finish in class, so we work on it at lunch, hunched over our books in the hallway in front of Paul's locker. When we finish, Paul pulls out a sandwich. "I like the picture you sent."

"Oh, thanks." I look down, pretending to erase something on the lab.

"Where was it from?"

"Oh, just the beach near my grandfather's house." We've never talked about personal stuff before. *Come on, Syd, make eye contact.* I force myself to look up.

"Can I send you another picture?" Paul asks.

I duck my head again, feeling the heat rush to my face. "Um, sure," I say. "I think I have to go now— get ready for my next class."

"What class is that?"

"Oh, this writing thing." I start piling up my books.

"I didn't know you did that."

"It's just an elective," I say. Why can't I casually say, *Yeah, I like writing*? I'm not even sure if that's true. I don't know why Paul's bothering to talk to me at all. There are lots of cute girls in his crowd, Chinese girls with great outfits and long shiny hair. There's one girl I sometimes see talking to Paul who has gorgeous hair and a Hello Kitty phone case.

"I'm taking photography," Paul says as we stand up.

I feel some of the heat leave my face now that we're not talking about me. "Oh," I say, hugging my books to my chest. "That explains the photos."

Paul cracks his knuckles. "Those weren't my best ones." We start walking down the hall together. "I like taking close-up shots better."

"Like portraits?"

"No, more nature stuff." Paul looks sheepish.

"Oh." I'm not sure what to say about that.

"I could send you another picture, one of my better ones."

I glance up at Paul. He looks almost as embarrassed as me. I forget my own discomfort for a moment. He's a lot taller than I thought. I'm used to sitting next to him, and he's shorter when we're at a lab bench. For a moment we look at each other, and then neither of us is sure what to do. I must be the most awkward person on earth, and Paul is going to see that and never talk to me again. "Yes," I finally say, "send me more pictures."

Paul looks relieved. "You could send me some back."

"I'm not taking photography."

"Then send me something you've written."

I shake my head.

"Then send me a photo from your biking."

I'm not sure how he knows I bike, but I smile. "Okay." I take a step back. "I think I need to go now."

Paul waves goodbye, and I walk away from him and head back to my locker. Sofia is sitting on the floor with her phone. She looks up at me when I settle next to her. I feel strangely exhausted, like I've been fighting with someone instead of just talking to Paul.

"Where were you?" Sofia asks. "I was looking for you."

"Oh, I was finishing a chem lab with Paul."

Sofia tilts her head to the side. "That's so cute."

I let my head rest on Sofia's shoulder, and then I pull up Paul's cloud picture from earlier in the week. "He also sent me this."

Sofia slides her arm around me. "I told you he likes you."

"It's just a picture."

Sofia sighs. "He's totally courting you. It's so chivalrous."

I shake my head. Sofia reads too many Harlequins. "Why would he do that? He's my lab partner."

"Syd, don't be thick. He likes you. He probably thinks you're hot."

"I'm not hot."

She elbows me in the ribs. "You are too."

"No, look at me. I'm not hot."

Sofia pretends to frame my face with her hands. "You're, like, model material."

"Model material?"

"You know, skinny girls."

"I'm not model skinny."

"Okay, so you're not exactly *Vogue* cover material, but maybe he's into strong, muscular girls."

"That doesn't sound so attractive."

"Are we going to go down this road again? Because if you need your ego pumped and a makeover to go with it, I can do that." Sofia tosses her head. "You have amazing legs, great cheekbones, a beautiful neck and the straightest, whitest teeth I've ever seen. Maybe you should smile a little and show them off." I flash Sofia a grin. She pokes me in the arm and then strokes my hair. "You also have a cute haircut."

Sofia recently suggested I get my hair styled with bangs and layers at the front. She also helped me dye it auburn instead of its natural mousy brown. I like the cut because my bangs are long enough that I can hide behind them if I want to.

Sofia continues, "Paul likes you—let's leave it at that. You should send him a cloud back."

I take a picture of the pink suede ballet flats I've worn all week and send the photo to Sofia. "I'm courting you," I tell Sofia when she gets the photo.

Sofia ignores me and sighs. "I think it's sweet you're texting each other. Maybe you'll even go on a date."

I frown. "I'd never survive that." Even the thought of a date makes me queasy.

"You'd be fine."

"No, if it's more than homework, we'd have to talk to each other."

"You can talk to people. You talk to Fen and me, right? Besides, a date sounds so romantic." She wrinkles up her nose. "Everyone else just hooks up at parties."

"We're not dating. We're just doing homework together."

Sofia grins at me. "We'll see what kind of homework you do next time."

"Sofia…"

"Yeah?"

I want to tell her that I don't even know how to kiss, but Sofia's the kind of friend who would probably make me practice on her, so I leave it.

"What?" Sofia says again.

"I'm just nervous. What if I don't like him that much?"

She shrugs. "Then you'll get a new lab partner."

I collapse against Sofia's shoulder again. She makes everything sound so easy.

⁓ ❧ ⁓

In writing class Mrs. Lee has us do a free-write called "I Believe." She says, "Don't worry about what you think that means, and don't edit as you go along or judge what you've written. Keep your pen moving, and if you go off on a memory or a tangent, keep going. Don't censor yourself. There's no right or wrong way to do this exercise, and we won't be sharing these, so you can write personal things." She nods, and everyone pulls out paper and pens or starts tapping away on personal devices. I pull out a journal I've been using for the course, a pink one with green hearts on the cover. I sigh. What do I believe?

I believe in climate change, environmental degradation, the devastation of our pine forests, market indexes, biking, the power of the Internet, dentistry, grass, moss etched in sidewalks, rain, fog, dew, my shadow, the power of positive thinking (sometimes), cashmere sweater sets, patent leather shoes, Coach purses, concealer, Maybelline Volum' Express Mega Plush mascara, pearls, pine nuts, pesto, bread pudding, steak, pinot grigio (not that I've tried any yet) and heirloom tomatoes. I also believe in all-white furnishings, retro kitchens and hardwood floors.

I could go on, but Mrs. Lee switches the activity. "Now write what you don't believe in. This is a way to flip your thinking, to get your brain to go somewhere different."

This is harder. I have to tap my pen for a few minutes before I start writing. *I don't believe in corduroy or crushed velvet or scarves. I also don't believe in sweet pickles, sherbet (except between courses), pretzels or baked potatoes. I don't believe in rouge, butterfly clips or roughing it. I also don't believe in singing for your health or spirit, guitars or "Kumbaya." I don't believe in monsters, fairies, ghosts, heaven or hell, life after death or God. I don't believe in beer, nacho chips, Cheezies or putting your hand up in class. I don't believe in sharing what you write, unless you have to.*

At the end of class Mrs. Lee says we should start thinking about poetry and reading the poems she's assigned for the course. She says maybe we'll get a poem out of our free-write today. When I glance back through my writing, I don't see how.

While walking to Mandarin class, I get a text from Paul. He's sent another picture, this time of a white fleshy mushroom with a pointed head and dirt and water droplets clinging to it. It's a great picture but a really ugly mushroom. And it's…a mushroom.

Great pic, I write back. I'm not sure what else to say.

Thanks. Your turn.

I'll think about it. But when I do, I'm not even sure where to start.

After school I decide to visit Zeyda again, to surprise him and maybe convince him to go to the JCC with Crystal. Also, the weather has improved. It's not exactly beautiful, but the sky has cleared, and you can see patches of blue. It's a relief to ride in dry weather.

When I arrive at Zeyda's, he barely turns to look at me.

"Your zeyda is in a bad mood because he had a fight with your mother," Crystal explains.

I plunk down beside Zeyda and give his hand a squeeze. "What else is new?"

Zeyda doesn't even look up.

Crystal hovers in front of us. "She wants him to go to your house for some special meal?"

"Oh, Passover," I say.

"It should be here," Zeyda grumbles.

"You're going to lose this one, Zeyda. She has it all planned out."

Zeyda looks up. "I always lead the Seder."

"Well, Mom's got a different vision."

Zeyda crosses his arms against his chest. "I might not come."

"Your loss," I say. "But we'll miss you. Anyway, it's more than a month away. Maybe she'll decide it's too much work and change her mind." I know this isn't going to happen.

Zeyda glares at me. "Once your mother gets something in her mind, it doesn't go away. It buzzes there like a bee until she makes a big mess of things."

Or she gets her MBA or organizes a spectacular fundraiser for the hospital or plans an amazing but touchy-feely Seder. I squeeze Zeyda's hand. "I brought you something."

"What's that?"

I pull the JCC catalog out of my backpack and flip to the page I marked. "Look, there's a seniors' drop-in group on Wednesdays."

"So?" Zeyda's eyebrows rise so far up his wrinkled forehead they almost reach his receding hairline.

"So I was thinking maybe you and Crystal could go together. Make it a date." I wink at Crystal.

"I like a date," Crystal says. "What do they do there?"

"Some games, sometimes dancing."

Crystal twirls. "Ooh, sounds nice, Morris. Take me dancing."

Zeyda scrunches up his face. "It doesn't sound nice. It sounds awful."

"Oh, Zeyda, don't be such a grouch," I say.

"That's my job now."

Crystal throws up her hands. "Maybe they have cards. Maybe you could play poker with friends instead of strangers, like at the casino."

I chime in. "Mom says her friend Carol Sandler's father, Abe, goes. You know him from shul, don't you?"

"Ach, then I'd have to listen to him talk about his big lawyer days."

"So," I shoot back, "you can brag about being a hotshot day trader."

"Abe Sandler can't even walk. He's a cripple! Why would I want to talk to him?"

"Morris," Crystal says, sounding disapproving. "That's not a nice thing to say."

"You don't walk very fast yourself," I point out. Crystal giggles, and Zeyda harrumphs.

Crystal goes to make Zeyda's dinner, and I distract him from his gloom by pulling up the TSX site on his tablet so he can show me his trades. He gets a little excited when he sees Exxon is up twenty points. When I ask about the moral implications of investing in oil when we're fighting global warming, Zeyda stares at me. "Do you want to make money or save the world?" Then he launches into a long lecture about mining sites in Canada and the possibility of 6 percent interest. I try to follow as best I can.

After Zeyda goes over my list of investments for the contest, he taps my phone. "How is your boyfriend? Still sending you pictures?"

"He's just a friend."

"In my day you didn't send a girl pictures on her cell phone unless you had something in mind."

I fight a blush, imagining Zeyda thinking of something romantic. "In your day there were no cell phones."

"True. Fine. The equivalent then."

"Which was what?"

"Well…" Zeyda thinks about it. "Talking on the phone. Your mother used to talk on the telephone all the time.

THE MOST DANGEROUS THING

And she still does. Yak, yak, yak, all day. And your bubbie, I took her to the movies."

"That's called dating, right?"

Zeyda lifts one eyebrow. "Young people don't do that anymore?"

I think about Sofia's comment about people hooking up. "Not so much. There's just this, I think." I hold up my phone.

"Is he still sending you clouds?"

"No," I say. "I got a mushroom."

Zeyda shakes his head. "What kind of guy is this?"

I grin. "I don't know."

"You know, if you had a nice Jewish boyfriend, he probably wouldn't be sending you clouds and weird mushrooms on your phone."

I ignore the part about the boyfriend being Jewish. "Oh? What would he send?"

Zeyda thinks about this for a couple of seconds. "A nice boy sends you real flowers. Maybe some jewelry."

I can't help myself. I smile. "Like a Venus flytrap?"

"A what?"

"It's this flower that eats flies. It's a carnivorous plant."

Zeyda shakes his head. "No wonder the whole world is getting divorced. They don't even know how to send flowers!"

"What does a girl send back?" I haven't sent Paul a photo today.

"A girl sends her heart, of course," Zeyda says.

I shake my head. This is the dumbest, most ridiculous and sexist thing I've heard in at least a week. Why would you give your heart away for some dumb flowers you could buy yourself at the grocery store? And is your body supposed to follow along after your heart? There's no point in saying this to Zeyda—he's just trying to be romantic, even if it's so old-fashioned it's sexist. I shake my head. "You know," I say, "if you went to the JCC, you might meet someone, maybe someone you could send real flowers to. That might be kind of exciting. I bet there's a ton of single women at those things."

Zeyda's face falls. "Ah, Sydney, none of them would be half as beautiful or witty or charming as your bubbie."

I squeeze Zeyda's hand. It's true. Before Bubbie got sick, she was an amazing person. Maybe not witty, like Zeyda claims, but charming and beautiful. Bubbie made homemaking an art form. She was a great cook, shopper and decorator. She was always planning a party or making a cake for someone else's party. She would have made a fantastic event planner if she had lived at a time when women like her had careers.

Neither Zeyda nor I say anything for a while, each of us wrapped up in our memories of Bubbie. I feel a blanket of sadness settle over Zeyda. It's like his own fog, except his has a name and a reason, unlike my own. The sky darkens and the living room grows dim. Neither of us mentions turning on the lamps, and Zeyda and I sit in the gloom a long time. Finally I say, "Let's go for a walk."

"I haven't been yet today," Zeyda admits.

"You should. Fresh air," I say. I want to add *to clear our minds*, but it seems weird to say out loud. I kiss Zeyda's cheek instead. I pull on my jacket and then help Zeyda with his hat and coat. I tell Crystal we're going out for a bit.

I wheel Zeyda down the gentle slope of his driveway and then west, past the park. It's twilight, the lights of downtown coming on. Abby and I used to think Zeyda and Bubbie owned the park, since they didn't have a yard at their house. We used to call it Zeyda and Bubbie's Park. We played tea party in the bushes and had contests to see who could jump off the swings from the highest point. I'd like to stop at the swings now, but Zeyda needs to be near the ocean, to not just watch it from his window but feel it on his cheeks.

I push him along the beach path. To the left is a grassy park dotted with massive willows, and then the cliffs up to the University Endowment Lands. To the right is the beach with its neat rows of logs. In the distance I can make out the North Shore mountains, and downtown twinkling off to the side. No one is on the path except a few dedicated joggers in hats and mittens. The tide is still in, and the ocean is splashing up high on the sand. Zeyda and I stop at the lookout near the sailing club, the wind blowing against us. I can just make out the shape of the mountains against the dark sky. I take out my phone and snap a picture. Maybe I'll send that to Paul.

The container ships sound their foghorns. "I love that sound," Zeyda says, "but usually I'm hearing it from my bed, not out here in the wind."

"Are you cold?" I ask.

"No, I'm good," Zeyda says.

My phone buzzes in my pocket a few times, but I ignore it. The night is too beautiful to look at a screen. Zeyda and I stay a few minutes longer, and then I wheel him back.

It's completely dark when we get home, and Crystal is waiting in the entry, looking worried. "You were gone so long. What were you doing out there?"

Zeyda says, "We needed some fresh air. It was good to feel the dark."

I'm surprised by Zeyda's words, but Crystal is already clucking and helping him off with his coat and hat. "Ooh, Sydney, your dad called looking for you. He's going to pick you up."

"My dad?" Dad works downtown or on building sites around the Lower Mainland. He usually bikes if it's not too far away. He's working in Burnaby right now, nowhere near here.

"Yes. He said he was texting you."

Dad never texts me. Still, when I pull out my phone there's a text from him. He wrote, **U still at Z's?**

Yes, I type.

Ride home tog?

Sure.

But where is he coming from?

Crystal wheels Zeyda into the living room and gives him his evening Scotch and bowl of nut mix. While I'm waiting for Dad, I send Paul the photo of the mountains and sky. I hit *Send* quickly, before I can change my mind. I look at the picture again, then write on my phone,

no stars yet,

but they're coming,

pinpricks on velvet,

we are not alone

I almost send Paul the poem too, but he might think it too weird or think it's about him. I shove my phone into my bag.

A few minutes later Dad rings the bell, his long legs still straddling his bike. He's wearing his biking gear instead of his work clothes, and his graying beard looks sweaty, like he's been on his bike a while already. "Hi, Morris," he calls into the house as I gather my things.

Zeyda yells back, "How're the bridges?" He asks Dad the same question every time he sees him.

"Holding up fine," Dad calls back.

"Good, good to hear," Zeyda says.

"Naomi said to ask you about Friday-night dinner again. We could pick you up or call a taxi for you. Whichever you prefer."

Zeyda bats a hand in the air. "It's not for me, all that singing and food." Zeyda has boycotted our Friday-night dinners ever since Mom joined a new shul, made some new friends and, in her words, revitalized our Shabbat dinners. I think he also hates having us help him navigate the front stairs of our house.

Dad shrugs. "I said I would try. Maybe next week."

Zeyda doesn't say anything else, so I bend down to give him a hug. "See you soon," I say. I feel like telling him how sometimes being with Paul lifts the fog, if only temporarily, but who is Zeyda going to be with? No one, unless he gets himself to the seniors' drop-in.

"Come back soon," he says. "I'll teach you about market equities."

"Okay. And think about the JCC."

"What's happening there?" Dad calls from the front door.

"Lots of single women." I turn back to Zeyda. "Think about it."

Zeyda frowns at me. "Get out of here. Go ride your bike in the dark like a crazy person, with your crazy father."

"I heard that," Dad says. "It's the closest thing to flying I've found."

Yes, flying, I think. Sometimes.

"Goodbye, David, Goodbye, Sydney." Zeyda dismisses us.

Outside, Dad waits while I unlock my bike and fasten my helmet.

"How come you were over this way tonight?" I ask as I switch on my bike lights.

"I have a new volunteer position."

"Really?" Usually Dad doesn't do that kind of thing.

"Yep. At the AIDS hospice."

I strap on my helmet. "Does their building need structural repairs or something?"

Dad laughs. "No, I was inside."

I raise my eyebrows. "Like, visiting with sick people?"

Dad nods. "You want to take the long way home? It's faster."

He means up the hill to the university campus and then along the bike path on Eighteenth, where there's less traffic. "Sure," I say, then, "Why were you visiting with sick people?"

"I told you, it's my new volunteer position."

I get on my bike, and Dad and I head out to the street. "But you hate sick people." Dad can't stand hospitals. He used to break into a sweat when we visited Zeyda after his stroke. He doesn't even like to pick up Mom at work.

"I don't hate sick people," Dad says evenly. "Tonight I was helping feed people who are ill." We're coasting along the beach road now. Dad's ready to go faster, his legs already warmed up, but he's letting me set the pace before we hit the hill.

"You've never had anything to do with sick people before," I say.

"That's true. I guess I'm trying to reach out, do something different."

"Oh. That's weird."

There's definitely something else going on here, but all Dad says is "You ready to fly?"

I nod, and Dad pulls ahead. I lift out of the saddle, pumping my legs to keep up. Slowly we build up speed to take on the hill.

After dinner Abby and I are loading the dishwasher while Mom and Dad figure out some bills. Abby is singing her way through *Les Misérables* and dripping water all over the floor.

"Why are you so happy?" I ask.

"I'm excited about the monologues." She whips a dishtowel through the air.

"Oh, did the admin approve the play?"

"They need to see the final script."

"So?"

"We're working on it."

"Isn't it already written?" I pass Abby a pot to scrub.

"Yes, but some of us are writing our own monologues. I hadn't planned on it, but there's this guy, Jay—well, everyone thinks he's a guy, but he wants to be a girl—and he asked to be in it because he wants to write a trans monologue about wanting a vagina."

"Wow." I stop slotting knives into the dishwasher and look up at Abby.

"Yeah. Wow. I had to think about that. Some of the other girls weren't even sure about having a guy in the play. I mean, this is about women, right? But then we'd be some sort of horrible oppressive matriarchy or, I don't know, a coven of mean girls if we didn't let in someone who wanted to be a girl, right? Anyway, he wrote this amazing piece about wanting to have a woman's body. How could we say no? Then once Jay wrote his own piece—I still don't know if I'm supposed to say *he*, *she* or *they*, but I'm going to ask tomorrow— a whole bunch of us decided to write our own monologues. I don't think we'll be able to call it *The Vagina Monologues* anymore, because that's trademarked, but we'll be able to call it something similar, like *The Vagina Stories* or *The Vagina Musings* or *Down Under* or something like that."

I can't help myself. "What's your monologue going to be about?" I brace myself and imagine the worst. She's probably going to describe periods or sex.

"I'm going to write about all the things we call the vagina instead of vagina."

This doesn't sound so bad. "Like hoo-haw?"

Abby giggles. "I forgot about that one. No, I'm going to write about taking back the word *cunt*."

I close the dishwasher and back away from Abby. "You're kidding, right?"

"No."

My hands come up to my cheeks. "What do you mean, *taking it back*? That's, like, the worst word for girl parts I can think of."

"Wait a second." Abby goes to the back door and pulls a book out of her backpack with the c-word written right across the cover. "No, look at this. I found it in with Mom's old women's studies books, and it says that *cunt* was an old Germanic word, and that people have started using it as a swearword, but that actually it's really powerful. There's a short section in the original play about the word *cunt* and the letters, but it doesn't talk about the word the way I want to."

Of course Mom would have a book called *Cunt* in her collection. Doesn't every mother? Or maybe only a mom whose idea of a fun car quiz game involves naming the parts of the vagina. Last summer when our drive to the Okanagan was getting long and boring, Mom turned down the radio and announced we were going to play a game. For five points, she had said to Abby and me, who knows the proper term for female external genitalia?

I know! Abby yelled. The vulva!

Excellent, Mom said. Okay, here's a question for you, Syd. True or false: if your period is late, you must be pregnant.

I slunk lower in my seat. I'm not playing.

False, Abby crowed. False! You might be stressed, or sick, or have malnutrition.

Correct. Another five points.

Ask me a geography question, I grumbled.

Geography sounds good, Dad agreed.

I take the cunt book from Abby and silently mouth the title, feeling its power in my mouth. It's a word that doesn't take no for an answer. The hard *c* and the final *t*—you could hurl the word through the air and it might cut someone. It sounds like a swearword. I hate it. I turn to Abby. "There is no way the school is going to let you perform a monologue with that word in it."

"I might surprise everyone. You know, slip it in."

I shudder. That's so Abby. Sometimes I think she likes to be edgy just to get attention. I wouldn't sleep for a month if I had something like that planned, but Abby doesn't seem to be breaking a sweat. "How much trouble will you be in then?" I ask.

"I don't think they'll kick me out of school, but if they did, wouldn't that be awesome? When people asked me why I had to change schools or start homeschooling, I could say it was because I was taking back the word *cunt* to give power to women's bodies. I could say I was challenging the patriarchal structure of our world." Abby does a pirouette, landing dramatically with her hands above her head.

I shake my head. "You're crazy."

I leave Abby dancing in the kitchen and head downstairs to do some homework. After I work through my calculus, I think about Abby writing a c-word monologue and then about Zeyda, who thinks flowers are the way to a girl's heart and her body too. The c word makes me think of vaginas as weapons, like something that says, *Take that!* Cunt rhymes with lots of words—bunt, runt, hunt, stunt, grunt—but I'm not sure how to make these into a poem. I sigh. I don't need to rename my body parts to protect myself. I never let anyone close enough to hurt me.

Four

THE FOG BUILDS ALL WEEK. I fall into bed by 9:00 PM, feeling as if dark clouds are swamping my brain. Each night the heaviness that overtakes me as soon as I lie down is more extreme. Sleep comes with a dull, heavy tug, and I wonder if I'll be able to get up the next morning. I plan new ways to get out of bed. Wednesday night I leave my phone in the bathroom, so that when I wake up Thursday morning I have to get up to see if Paul has texted me. He hasn't, and I feel myself shrivel a little, rooted to the cold tile floor. I stand in the bathroom with my phone in my hand and my head pressed against the mirror before I convince myself that if I don't get going, I'll have to go to school with my hair unwashed. Paul and I sit together in class that day, but the chem teacher lectures and then shows a video, so we don't talk. All day I check my phone, but there are no messages from Paul. I feel myself slowly start to deflate as the darkness tunnels into my chest.

Friday is the hardest day to get out of bed. Nothing works. Not Sudoku, not visualizing, not even leaving my phone in the bathroom. The effort of pushing the darkness away leaves me so exhausted that even choosing socks feels overwhelming. The darkness has seeped deep inside me, and it hurts to walk, to look at lights. I'm so late for school that Mom drives me, glaring at me the whole time while I pick at the banana muffin she grabbed for me on the way out. Worse, Paul is not at school. The fog feels as big as a rain cloud before a downpour. It's so bad I decide the week has gone on long enough. I leave school early and skip both writing and Mandarin.

At home I make myself some mint tea and then go downstairs. I'm about to head to my room when I hear giggling in the tent. I guess Abby has decided to skip class too. When I push back the curtain, she is sprawled on the cushions with her friend Sunita beside her. "Hey," I say.

Abby looks up at me. "Sunita and I are working on the play."

"Oh. Great." Usually the tent is just for us, but Abby's looking at me as if to say, *Do you mind?* Obviously I'm interrupting some deep discussion about women's bodies. I've seen Sunita and Abby at school together. Sunita is tiny with long black hair and big black eyes. She's part of a group of sassy, fearless twelfth-grade girls Abby hangs out with. They support the Gay-Straight Alliance and

Amnesty International, run for student council, hang out with the drama club and collect an assortment of odd guys, such as the boy who wears purple cowboy boots and eyeliner.

"I might go out for a bit," I say.

Abby nods, her attention on Sunita. "See you later."

I don't exactly leave. I go out the back door from the kitchen and down the porch steps, then sneak back in the basement door, which is on my side of the basement, so Abby can't hear me.

I quietly go into my room and open my closet door, step into the closet and close the door. Then I settle in the dark on the sheepskin rug I keep there, pull my knees up to my chest and close my eyes. Once my breathing slows, it's so quiet I can hear my heart beating. Then I can stop pretending not to be anxious, stop pretending the fog doesn't exist.

A deep relief comes over me. I let my face fall into the hangdog expression I've kept off it all day. I let my shoulders sag. My brain relaxes. No more chem or math, no more Sofia or Paul or Abby, no more pretending to be fine so people won't worry about me. There's only the gray haze of the fog. I don't bother shoving it away or pretending it's not there.

Every week I push myself, make myself study, take notes, eat, talk to people. It's very tiring, pretending to be normal. Sometimes I need an hour where I can stop. And the closet is good. Since no one knows where

I am, no one has to worry about me, and I don't have to pretend to be okay. I guess you could call sitting in the closet a kind of meditation, but it's different than the meditation techniques Dr. Spenser taught me—sadder and more of a relief. I try not to do it too often because one day I won't want to come out of the closet. One day I won't be *able* to come out of the closet. It will be too easy to be in there and too hard to be out.

I hear Mom come home around four, which is early for her, but it's Friday, and we have guests coming for dinner. I'm supposed to be making salad, not sitting in my closet. I hear Abby upstairs and Dad too. I should be helping, but the idea of our house full of guests makes me shrivel back into the corner. Minutes tick by and I still can't move. I try to imagine a bulb of light inside me, lightening my mood. When that doesn't work I focus on some wordplay. Mom's going to be mad I didn't make the salad yet. *Mother, other, not her, her here, her ear, ear, earlier, should have been.*

Then *Syd, the kid, Dad used to call me, that was easier, being a kid, now Syd the kid wants to get rid, of herself, at least for a while, this breathing body, this heavy brain.*

Composing something is one way to get out of the closet. I push open the door, roll onto the carpet and grab my phone to type the words before I forget them. Then I change into tights and my gray dress and comb my hair. I pull on my coat and shoes by the basement door, grab my backpack and then, after a few deep breaths, walk up the back steps and pretend to be getting home. It's almost five o'clock now.

The kitchen smells like freshly baked challah and chicken soup. Mom made the dough before work this morning, and Dad cooked the soup last night. Now Mom is peeling vegetables, and Abby is working on a cake. Dad is in our tiny front entrance, shoving shoes into the closet.

Mom glances at the clock on the microwave and frowns at me. "Where have you been?"

"Just studying with Sofia."

"Can you set the table, please?" She doesn't bother disguising the frustration in her voice. I can see she's already made the salad herself.

An hour later Mom's guests, mostly from the congregation at her new shul, arrive, including Miri and Todd Davis. The Davises are older than my parents, with grown-up children. Todd has unruly gray curly hair and dresses in these tunic-like hippie shirts that are embarrassing to look at. You'd think he'd be married to someone frumpy, but Miri Davis has the best clothes of any adult I've ever met, and her long black hair is always perfectly straight. Tonight she has on this gorgeous black skirt with gray silk threaded through it, ending in a gray-silk fringe above her knees, and a silky charcoal top that Sofia would die for. I sneak a picture of her jeweled open-toed pumps resting by the front door to send to Sofia.

Mom calls us all to the table, and we gather around, Abby, Dad and me in our usual spots with the guests fitting in between us. Friday nights we used to light the candles, bless the wine and challah and then eat, but recently Mom has gotten into being more Jewish. She joined the choir at her new shul, and now we have to sing all these songs before we get to the blessings. It's one thing to sing in shul or in a choir, but somehow singing in your own dining room is embarrassing. Apparently I'm the only one who feels this way, because everyone else closes their eyes and sings with passion.

I stare at the floor and feel angry with Abby. She's supposed to be my ally, supposed to giggle in the kitchen with me and mock everything, but she's out there singing her heart out. Abby likes all kinds of music, even religious songs—anything that gives her a chance to show off her voice. Right now she's harmonizing some ode to God with Mom. When it's finally over, Mom welcomes everyone to our house, to our Shabbat, and asks us to take a moment of silence to feel mindful and present before we welcome the Shabbat. Will this never be over? The moment of silence seems to stretch forever. Finally we sit down to eat. I'm not that hungry, not even for Dad's delicious chicken soup.

I keep a low profile throughout dinner, trying to be helpful by serving the main course and clearing plates at the end of the meal. I drizzle fruit compote over the almond-and-orange cake Abby made and pour the tea.

I'm hoping dinner will be over soon and the guests will leave, but before I've even cleared the dessert plates, Mom has her guitar out, and the guests are moving to the living room to sing some more. Mom says she has a new *niggun*, a wordless tune, to teach everyone. I hover by the doorway listening for a moment while everyone else raises their voices to God, to sing his or her praises. Does God even care if people sing his or her songs? Maybe s/he looks down and hears people singing and thinks, Suckers!

Mom comes over to me and squeezes my shoulder. She doesn't look mad at me anymore. "Hey," she says, "try and enjoy the music." I squirm under her hand. "You don't have to sing. Just be here with us and listen."

"Yeah, I don't think so." I take the opportunity to slink downstairs.

In my room I try listening to music on my phone, but I can still feel the house vibrating with everyone's joy. I think about the closet, but it won't dampen the music enough, so I put on a sweater, grab my phone and step into the backyard through the basement door. It has been raining, so everything is still damp, and my breath puffs in the air. I look up at the living-room lights, at the steamed windows. I can hear voices, and a shriek of laughter reaches me. I briefly see Mom in profile in the window, holding a wineglass, before she moves away. Part of me wants to head back inside and be part of that warmth and music, but I can't do it.

I have too much of Zeyda's sadness and my own inside me. Mom says music is another way to get out of yourself, but not for me.

Even the backyard feels claustrophobic with all the people singing and heating up our house, so I go out the back gate and start wandering down the lane. When I get to the end of our street, I cross the road and head down the next lane. I do this sometimes when I don't want to see anyone. There's a whole different world in the lanes. You can peer into people's backyards and sometimes see into their houses. People have fewer blinds on their back windows. I like to see people eating or watching TV. Once I stopped to watch two children playing with blocks. Now more of the houses have big garages and fences, so you can't see anything, and I like that too. Then the lane feels like a private space, a secret tunnel.

After a few blocks I check my messages. An hour ago, when we were eating dinner, Fen wrote, **Biking Sat am. Dad's @ 7.**

Perfect, I think. That'll get me out of bed tomorrow. I type back, **See you then.**

I'm about to put my phone back in my pocket when Paul writes, **I'm stuck on math question four.**

I stop in the lane. I don't believe Paul's stuck on question four, even if he wasn't at school today. I did it at lunch, and it wasn't tricky. I spin in a small circle, trying to decide what to write. Before I can make up my mind, Paul writes again: **Can u help me?**

I take a small breath and then type, **Yes.** Sofia would be proud of me for these three small letters.

Paul writes, **Tomorrow?**

No school tomorrow, I write back.

I know.

I inhale deeply. I'm not pretending anymore that Paul is sending me mushroom pictures for no reason. The seconds are ticking by and I need to respond, but I also want to take this moment in. I'm not even sure if I like Paul that way, but he likes me, and that's pretty awesome, even if it's crazy and maybe dangerous. I don't mean dangerous like Paul might be a serial killer. I mean dangerous like I'll have to talk to him or, I don't know, do the things Abby is talking about in her play.

Paul is waiting, waiting for me to write back, but I can't seem to do it. Finally I take another deep breath and write, **Busy Saturday, how about Sunday?** That way I can change my mind if I need to. That way I can think about it on my bike ride with Fen, and maybe it'll clear the fog for the rest of the weekend. And maybe it'll keep me out of the closet, because anything—anticipation, excitement, even dread and anxiety—is better than the closet.

Paul writes, **See you then.**

I write **Yes** again, and then I head home. It would be an exaggeration to say I skip home, but my pace is definitely faster. I stop for a brief moment to text Sofia. **Meeting P Sunday!** And she writes back, **Which shoes?** which is so ridiculous and Sofia-like that I almost laugh out loud. I write, **Suggestions?** We go back and forth, Sofia suggesting increasingly crazy and expensive footwear, none of which I own. For the first time in what seems like forever, my body feels like its old normal self, my brain so clear it's almost like little crystals of light are exploding in it.

My house is still full of people singing and talking. I don't want to join them, but I don't want to be alone in my room either. I decide to clean up the kitchen, to start loading the dishwasher. That way I can listen to the music without being right in the center of things and make up for not helping before dinner. Mom starts to sing "Tsur Mishelo," one of my least-unfavorite Shabbat songs, and I find myself humming along.

Five

IN THE MORNING I WAKE UP to a dim grayish light creeping around my blinds. The fog doesn't feel too bad, only a thin layer in my head that might melt if I can get up. "Go away, fog," I whisper, but it rests heavily against the backs of my eyeballs. I stay still a few minutes longer, letting it grow heavier and heavier. If I don't get up soon and push it away, I'll miss biking with Fen and spend the whole day stressing about seeing Paul tomorrow. The fog thickens, and I feel as if I might cry, but that would be letting it win. There's no time for Sudoku this morning. Instead I try one of Dr. Spenser's meditation strategies. When it doesn't work I try to imagine my body glowing like a lightbulb until I grow so bright the fog melts away. This is a little better. Finally, I think about meeting Paul tomorrow and then just count to three and roll myself out of bed and into my biking clothes.

Once I'm up and going, I can still feel the fog wanting to press me down, but I create a list of tasks I need to accomplish and I check them off as I go—eat cereal, brush teeth, pin back hair into a low ponytail, find helmet. I leave a note on the counter for Mom and go out the back door to get my bike from the garage before anyone else is awake. Outside, the sky is low, threatening rain, and there's a thick layer of fog socking in the mountains. It's as if the way I feel inside has leaked out and covered the city. Maybe it has. Maybe I am the weather, and people will know and scowl at me. *Get your problems out of my air*, they'll say. *Think some damn happy thoughts and get us some sun*. Or maybe the whole city's depressed, and the weather is dismal because of everyone's unhappy thoughts. A chicken-and-egg argument, I think. Still, there are flowers everywhere, and thanks to the rain, the grass is green, the trees are erupting into color, cherry blossoms drift over the sidewalks. Dad's mom in Winnipeg says there's still a foot of dirty snow covering the city. I guess things could be worse. I'd rather rain than snow. At least you can still ride here most of the winter.

It's a short ride to Fen's, just a few blocks north. Fen's dad is already loading bikes onto the rack of his SUV, and I silently hand him mine. I go in the back door and sit with Fen for a minute. He's eating eggs at the kitchen table, not talking yet because it's early. He raises a hand in greeting, and I wave back. I can hear his feet tapping under the table while the rest of him looks half asleep.

Fen and his dad throw water bottles and energy bars into the car. A few minutes later we're on the road heading out of the city.

Fen's parents are divorced, and Fen lives one week with his mom and one week with his dad. He hates both of them, but at least when he's with his dad there's biking. Fen's dad's parents live in Maple Ridge, an hour's drive out of the city, so that's where we're heading. It's very flat there, and you can ride around on quiet roads. Since neither Fen nor his dad are big on small talk, I listen to music on my phone, eyes closed. The fog factor now that I'm up and out isn't great, but it's not bad. And biking will blast it away.

Fen's dad parks in his parents' gravel driveway, and we get our bikes off the rack. The house is still dark, so we don't need to say hello until we get back. We clip into our pedals and start down the long, empty road, Fen's dad leading. I'll fall behind eventually, but I know the route now, and the shortcuts if the ride is too long, which it usually is. My wrists ache as I grip the handlebars, and my quads are wondering why I'm making them move this early in the morning. For the first two kilometers I wish I was back in bed. Why am I doing this anyway? Just to stop thinking about seeing Paul? Just to get rid of the fog?

After a few minutes my legs and wrists loosen up, and the rain that starts to splash against my bike glasses doesn't bother me. Fen's dad picks up the pace and lifts himself out of the saddle, Fen follows suit, and then so do I, determined to keep up even if they both have longer legs. I'm warm now, and I am no longer a body. I'm a machine, my legs pistons, my hips the cogs holding everything together. As my breathing quickens, my heart fills my blood with oxygen, blasting the fog out of my pores. My machine/body heats up, and the heat takes away any possibility of thought. There's only action, my legs pumping, my breath puffing into the cool morning damp.

We climb a small hill, pause to check for traffic and then coast down. Downhill used to be the hardest part, letting go, allowing myself to go fast, learning to lean into the curves. What if I wiped out? I worried about banging up my teeth. Now I'm used to the speed, and when I coast down the first hill, I feel the last of the fog evaporate. Then I lose myself in the motion. How fast can I go? How low can I crouch over the bike to reduce my wind resistance? How can I get my legs to go as fast as Fen's and his dad's? I keep up for the first hour, and then we stop for a short break. Fen's smiling now, his dad relaxed. They talk about gear, about the latest carbon composite bikes and how much they cost. I focus on eating, on refueling enough for the ride back. But it doesn't matter if I keep up. I've made my goal for this week. Besides, if I ride back with them, I'll probably have to make small talk with Fen's grandparents, and that is something I can do without.

I'm relaxed on the way back, Fen and his dad way out of sight. The weather is still gray, dismal, socked in, but I'm warm, soaked through with my own sweat, and inside I am a clear, light-blue color, maybe the same shade as Zeyda's eyes. It's a good color to be. I even feel excited about seeing Paul tomorrow. Maybe he'll text me another picture and I'll be able to look him in the eye when we meet.

When I get back, Fen and his dad are gorging on bacon, eggs and home fries, all made by Fen's grandma Fern. Fen's grandparents' house is almost as dated as Zeyda's, but in a totally different way. If Zeyda's house hasn't changed since 1985, then Fen's grandparents' house hasn't changed since 1975. The bungalow has wood paneling in the living room, a metal screen door that slams when you let it go and old wooden kitchen cupboards with scalloped edges. There's a country theme throughout the house—lots of checked pillows and lace curtains, and an old Formica table and vinyl-covered chairs. Fen's grandparents both look the same to me, with cropped gray hair and plaid shirts. The only major difference is that Fen's grandma stands by the stove, whereas Fen's grandfather never seems to be anywhere but at the table with a newspaper.

By the time I arrive in the kitchen, Fen and his dad are almost done eating, wiping the last of their eggs up with their toast. I stand by the screen door, stretching out my quads.

"What can I get you, Sydney?" Grandma Fern asks.

I hold up my water bottle. "I'm good, thanks."

"Not even a piece of toast?"

"Oh, no thanks," I say.

"Two hours of cycling and you're not hungry?" Grandma Fern shakes her head.

We have the same conversation every time I come. I can't eat so soon after biking, and even though we don't keep kosher, the smell of bacon always turns my stomach. Still, I like Fen's grandparents. They're totally unlike anyone I know. Grandma Fern raises chickens and has a huge vegetable garden. Grandpa Bill sometimes goes hunting or fishing, depending on the season. Grandma Fern has the same reddish complexion as Fen and his dad, and even though she's wrinkled and lumpy around the middle, you can tell she used to be a good athlete. At eighty-three she still swims three times a week and cross-country skis when her arthritis isn't acting up.

Grandma Fern is still fretting about me not eating, so I accept a peanut butter sandwich. Relief floods her face, and I feel better as the protein hits my system.

On the way home I'm damp but happy. I try to calculate how long the ride will keep the fog at bay. The afternoon for sure, and maybe into tomorrow morning if I'm lucky. Monday will be a whole new problem, but everyone feels crappy on Mondays, and I don't have a choice about getting out of bed on school days. There are people who can't even get out of bed, but I'm not going to be like that. I'm just not.

When I get home I lie in a hot bath, letting my mind blissfully wander. I think about the road out in Maple Ridge and the chickens in the yard and the clear streaks of yellow in the sky, where the horizon was just a field with no buildings. Maybe one day I'll take Paul out there.

Mom, Dad and Abby are preparing lunch as I'm getting out of the tub. I dry off, comb out my hair and pull on some leggings and a sweater. My body feels tired in a good, warm way—clean too. I join everyone in the kitchen.

Mom puts smoked salmon, cream cheese and some egg salad on the table. Dad's slicing bagels, and Abby's putting together a vegetable plate of tomatoes, onions and cucumbers.

"Are there any rugelach?" I ask.

"There are mun cookies." Mom points to the box on the sideboard.

Mun cookies, which are thin poppy-seed cookies, are my second favorite. I put the kettle on so we can dunk them in tea.

A few minutes later we sit down at the table. I'm absolutely starving now, the first time I've had a real appetite in days, and I heap my plate with veggies and a bagel and lox. I also help myself to some leftover *kugel* from last night.

When we're done eating, Abby excuses herself and Dad goes to read in the living room; it's just Mom and me at the table. I offer to clean up, since I didn't help make dinner last night.

"You left pretty early this morning," Mom says.

"I wanted to ride with Fen and his dad," I explain. I avoid looking at her. I can't explain why I need to go biking without telling Mom about the fog. If she knew, she'd never stop asking about it or worrying about it. "There's too much traffic to bike fast in the city," I add.

Mom looks me straight in the eye. "You know you can tell me if something is bothering you, right? And you can always go back to Dr. Spenser."

I manage to nod my head, and then I change the subject. "What are you up to this afternoon?"

Mom looks at me carefully before she starts putting away the food. "I thought I might choose Haggadahs for the Seder," she says.

"What do you mean?"

"If we're going to have a Seder, we need Haggadahs." She grins.

Haggadahs are the books people use for Passover. They have prayers in them and stories and songs and readings. At Zeyda's house we always used these really boring ones.

"You want new ones?" I ask.

"Yep. There are so many choices. Here, look." Mom dries her hands on a dishtowel and shows me a list on her iPad. "There's *The Family Haggadah. The Vegetarian Haggadah of the Liberated Lamb.* There's *The Feminist*

Haggadah. There's also one by someone who calls herself the Velveteen Rabbi, and there's even *The Bob Dylan Freedom Haggadah.*"

"No."

"Yes." Mom grins again. "You all get to sing 'The Times They Are A-Changin'.'"

"Please tell me you aren't going to choose that."

Mom scrolls down the page. "How about *A Socialist Haggadah for Our People?*"

I back away from Mom with my hands in the air. "Zeyda will love that. How about just a regular read-the-story, do-the-blessings, call-it-a-night Haggadah?"

"Oh, Syd, that sounds so boring."

"What's wrong with boring?"

Mom flaps a dishcloth at me. "A Seder does not have to be boring."

I close the dishwasher. "What are you leaning toward?"

"I found one with guitar chords for all the different songs, so I think I'll go with that."

"*The Musician's Haggadah?*"

"Something like that."

"I'll be sure to tell Zeyda all about it." I can't keep the sarcasm out of my voice.

"It's okay, Syd," Mom says. "I promise we won't sing any Bob Dylan songs."

And I guess that is something to be thankful for.

I feel restless for the rest of the afternoon. I think about texting Paul, asking where we'll meet tomorrow, but I can't. I try and do some homework instead. I work on a poem that won't come out right, and when I can't concentrate on it, I reorganize the spice drawer and then refold Abby's sweaters into neat piles for her. I want to straighten her desk too, but last time I did that I also alphabetized her books, which she had already grouped thematically.

What is it Paul and I are going to do? It's just a math date. But where? He didn't say. Even if I'm nervous, agitated almost, this is better than the fog. And under my nervousness is a layer of excitement. I didn't know I liked him more than as a friend. And now that he's interested in me, I do? I try and figure this out. He's nice and cute and smart, so why shouldn't I like him? It's more than that though—there's something exciting about being with him. I blush thinking about that. Heat surges through me, and goose bumps form down my arms. I duck my head even though no one is looking. Oh god, maybe I won't meet him tomorrow.

I pace around the basement for a moment. I need further distraction, so I ask Mom if I can make dinner. She happily gives me her debit card to buy groceries. Abby offers to help, and we plan the meal and walk to the store together. We decide to make grape leaves stuffed with lamb, pine nuts and currants, a roasted-cauliflower dish and tabbouleh. As we cook, Abby sings songs from *The Sound of Music* and tries to get me to join in. I hum a bit of "Edelweiss" with her. Dinner is delicious, and I manage to distract myself until about nine o'clock.

Then I start debating whether I should text Paul or not. The indecision is so dumb, I start to hate myself. My body is tired from biking, but my mind buzzes with anxious questions about seeing him tomorrow, and I lie in bed wide awake. Where are we going tomorrow? Are we really going to work on math problems, or are we going to do something else? When I imagine Paul and me standing close enough to kiss, what his lips would feel like against mine, I feel even more restless. I get up and slump into a beanbag chair in the tent.

Abby joins me, wearing pajamas printed with cupcakes. "I didn't know you were still up," she says.

"I'm too restless to sleep," I say.

"Why?" she asks.

"I don't know." I want to tell Abby about Paul, but I need to keep it private, in case things don't work out or something embarrassing happens.

Abby narrows her eyes. "You're such a liar."

I groan. "Fine. I'm waiting for a text from someone."

Abby's eyes widen. "Ooh, that sounds interesting."

"It's stressful."

"A text from someone you like?" Abby leans toward me, her eyes wide.

I sigh. "If you ask me a lot of questions, I'll be even more stressed, so if you want to help me, please don't."

Abby leans back. "Okay, I get it. No prying. So did you text him and he's not texting you back?"

"No, I'm just waiting."

Abby rubs her forehead in exasperation. "That's dumb. Does he know you're waiting?"

I hesitate. "Maybe."

Abby raises her eyebrows at me. "Hello? Send him something."

I take my phone out of my pajama pocket and type, **What time tomorrow?**

10 am? he writes back.

Great.

Details tomorrow.

Abby looks at me expectantly. "Better now?"

"Yes," I say.

"You're not going to tell me anything else?"

"No."

Abby rolls her eyes and lets herself flop back on the cushions. "You're impossible."

"I know." I bounce my legs. "I'm never going to be able to sleep."

Abby sits up and pulls out her phone. "Here, let me find something to entertain you." She flicks a few buttons on her phone and pulls up a video montage of dance scenes from movies. Abby plays video after video, adding commentary to the joyous movement, until my eyes start to close and I stumble to bed.

In the morning I expect to hear rain tapping into the gutters and then gurgling through the downspouts. Instead, thin sunshine makes each blade of grass on the lawn sparkle. I take an inventory of how I feel. My eyes open easily and I feel almost normal, except that I'm nervous about seeing Paul. My fog is lost in Maple Ridge. I sigh with relief.

The only reason to turn on my phone this morning is to check my messages. Paul has texted, **Clear skies, high clouds, light wind.**

I'm not sure what this means, but I type back, **Sounds good.**

Meet at the bus stop at 25th and Main.

Where to?

Surprise. Dress warmly.

I'm not sure what to do with this, so I pull on fleece-lined running tights and a warm sweater and throw some rain pants in my backpack.

Paul is waiting for me at the bus stop, wearing jeans and a rain jacket and carrying a large backpack. He grins when he sees me, and I smile back without even thinking about it.

"So where are we going?" I ask.

"You'll see."

"You're still not going to tell me?"

"It'll sound weird if I tell you. Just wait."

"I take it we're not doing math questions."

"Oh, I figured the math out. I thought we could do something else." I must look freaked because Paul adds, "Don't worry. The worst thing you'll say is that it's boring."

The bus comes a few minutes later, and we ride west until we get off at Oak Street. The properties are bigger than in my neighborhood, with lots of newer houses squished between older bungalows. Paul guides me past the high school at 33rd and Oak and up a steep path to a field I've never noticed before, even though I've been up and down Oak Street a zillion times. The field, a stretch of lawn punctuated with fir trees and high grass, stretches several blocks.

"I didn't know there was a park here," I say.

"Yeah, the trees block the view from the street. That's why I like this place. And watch this." Paul steps into the high grass, takes a tarp and a gray wool blanket out of his backpack and spreads them on the ground. He lies down on the blanket, and he's instantly hidden in the grass. I'm impressed by how casually he arranges his body, his hands tucked behind his head. Most people wouldn't notice this, but if you're a self-conscious person like me, you take note. The way Paul crouches down and then shoots his legs forward, his back descending at the same time, ending with his hands behind his head...it's like a dance. I almost want to ask him to do it again.

"What are we doing here?" I ask.

"Well, it's a beautiful day, clear skies, but windy." He points up at the sky. "I've always wanted to cloud-watch in this field."

"Oh." I can't help smiling. "Cloud watching?" My shoulders relax, and I look at Paul.

"Don't look at me—look up." He points again to the sky.

I tilt my head back. I can't remember the last time I looked at the sky. Thin high clouds waft across the blue, forming shapes and then breaking apart quickly. I get dizzy with my head tipped back, and Paul says, "Here, lie down."

I hesitate a moment. I'm not sure I can lie in a field with a boy, with Paul, hidden in the grass where no one can see us.

"Just a second," I say. "I want to look around."

Paul patiently waits while I walk through the high grass, turning in a circle to take in the surroundings—the trees that edge the field, the thin noise of the traffic on Oak Street. At the far end of the field a man has let his German shepherd off leash and is throwing a ball for the dog to chase. I let myself become distracted by the way the dog leaps across the field. I turn back to Paul, who I can tell is a little weirded out that I haven't joined him.

C'mon, Sydney, this is Paul, who you like, and he's planned this...this date for you. You can do this. And so I do. It's like moving in slow motion, but I walk back to the blanket and sit with my knees to my chest, and then I lie down next to Paul. I let my bangs fall into my eyes to hide me for a minute, and then I brush them aside. We look at each other for a moment and then back at the sky. Paul reaches for my hand and gives it a squeeze. His hand feels soft and warm and the right size to fit into mine, and even though my heart is exploding, I keep holding his hand and force myself to focus on the sky.

I haven't held anyone's hand in four years, maybe longer. The last time I let Mom and Dad hug me was when I graduated from seventh grade. They know being touched freaks me out, so Mom just blows me kisses every now and then, and sometimes Dad grabs the top of my head and kisses it. I can tolerate that because it's kind of like wrestling and not emotional. If they want someone to hug and kiss, they hug Abby. She likes that kind of thing.

For a few minutes I'm so nervous holding Paul's hand that I can barely take in what I'm seeing, but then I slowly become absorbed in the blue vastness of the sky, the ever-changing clouds, zipping free and light. They slide into new shapes before I can identify them, a cow becoming a goat, then a dog and then nothing, the sky a constant display of movement. At the edges of my vision I can see a few tree branches, bright with new leaves. All around us the grass rises, as if we are lying in an open-air tent. No one can see us unless they are standing right beside us. I feel my body sink into the earth, feel the cold hardness beneath me, cushioned by the springiness of the bent grass. A twig jabs one heel. Beside me Paul breathes, slowly and calmly, and after a while I feel my own breath match his. A shiver runs through me, and Paul turns to me.

"Cold?"

I shake my head. I want to say, "Just happy." I smile instead. I didn't know that I wanted this, but now that I have it, it feels right, like I don't have to be worried about it. This is Paul and me. Paul squeezes my hand again and somehow we lie closer together, the sides of our bodies pressed against each other. I feel my heart start to race, and I think I might not be able to deal with this, so I take a few deep breaths. This is the opposite of the closet—this is feeling light and happy. Maybe this is a way out of the fog. I can't imagine it ever descending again, being overwhelmed with that heaviness, not while lying here next to Paul. And if it does come back, I'll think about this moment. I exhale a long satisfied breath.

Slowly I forget about Paul, and even the field, and the distant traffic and buses. I only see the sky, and then words start to form in my head, in long chains: *cloud, sky, fly high, fly high in the sky, little cloud, long and thin, and now you are changing shape, letting the elements break you down, build you up.* I sit up and pull my phone out of my pocket and start jotting down words. Most of it is crap, but it doesn't matter—I might find a few words I like later.

While I write, Paul takes pictures of the sky with his phone. After a few minutes he pokes my leg. "Are you writing for your class?"

I nod.

"Oh. Can I hear something?"

"Uh, I don't think so."

"Okay." Paul lies back down. I try to pick up where I left off, but I'm feeling self-conscious now, so I put my phone away and lie back down on the blanket. Paul's hand finds mine again, and this time it doesn't freak me out as much.

Paul turns to me. "Thanks for coming."

"Thanks for inviting me," I manage to say. Our faces are so close together I can see Paul's individual eyelashes, the way they outline his dark eyes. There's a pause when neither of us says anything, and it feels like a moment when we're supposed to kiss, so I move a tiny bit away and prop myself up on one elbow. "How come you weren't in class on Friday?"

Paul exhales and lets his hands come over his eyes, his forehead wrinkling. "My dad was in town, and he wanted me to spend the day with him."

"Oh, where does he live?"

"Hong Kong."

"You got to miss school?"

"Yeah."

"That sounds like fun."

Paul sighs. "It wasn't."

"What did you do?"

Paul sits up, his body hunched over his knees and his fingers worrying the edge of the blanket. "He wanted me to come to this business meeting he had, and then we had to go to this lunch with a bunch of people all talking and eating at once, and then we went to look at some development project he's invested in, in Burnaby."

"Oh, that does sound kinda crappy."

"Yeah, he's always trying to get me interested in his business plans."

I sit up so I'm across from Paul, my legs crossed. If I had a day with Dad, we'd go biking; with Mom it would be lunch and something cultural, like an art show or dance performance. "What would you like to have done instead?"

Paul thinks about this for a minute. "Well, I like this." He gestures around. "Nature stuff. There's this ancient forest on Vancouver Island I'd like to see. They have amazing banana slugs and massive mushrooms."

"Would your dad be into that?"

Paul raises his eyebrows. "Definitely not. I might get to go with my sister, Julie, this summer."

I nod. "That sounds good."

Neither of us says anything for a moment, and I feel like Paul might kiss me and I can't decide how I feel about this. He's holding my hand again, resting it on top of his knees, and I'm not sure how that happened.

And then Paul leans forward and kisses me lightly on the lips, and I'm so stunned I freeze. The kiss only lasts a moment, and I open my eyes, amazed that I am still whole on the blanket, blood coursing through me, my eyes shining like stars, tips of my fingers and toes tingling. He kisses me again, for longer this time, and I feel like I could stay here all day with the breeze blowing over us and me inhaling the good smell of Paul's shirt and skin.

Six

ON MONDAY MORNING I WAKE UP with a smile on my face.
My body feels light, and there's a song playing in my
head, *Paul, Paul, Paul!* like the bird I sometimes hear on
clear days from the pear tree in the yard. I reach for my
phone, not because I need Sudoku, but in case there's a
text from Paul. There is. He's written, **Good morning.**

See you soon, I write back.

Yes, it's a good morning, even if it's pouring outside.
The sky is low and gray, and the wind whips the rain
against the house in wild bursts. Even Dad isn't biking
this morning. Mom offers to drive Abby and me if we
hurry. We bustle around, quickly making lunches and
gulping down breakfast. I borrow a hot-pink miniskirt
from Abby to wear over black tights, with a silky black
sweater and silver flats. It's a lot of color for me, that skirt,
but it shows how I feel.

Because Mom drops us off at school, I have a few minutes before classes start, and I go to my locker. Usually I arrive with just enough time to get to first class. "Good morning, everyone," I sing to Sofia and Fen.

"Hey, you're early," Sofia says. "How come?"

I give her a kiss on the cheek. "Because of the gorgeous weather."

"What's with you?" Fen stares at me. "You don't usually even talk until Tuesday." I sidestep around him to undo my lock. Fen turns to Sofia. "Now she's dancing on a Monday morning?" He blocks my locker. "Did you win the lottery or something?"

Sofia kicks him in the shins. "No, goofball, she saw a boy on the weekend."

"Did she, like, talk to him too?" Fen says.

"Ouch," I say. "I talk to boys. I talk to you."

"I don't count," Fen says, which makes Sofia and me smile.

"Hey, you know what I mean," Fen protests.

"Fenny doesn't count," Sofia singsongs.

Fen ignores her and says, "Who is making you capable of talking on a horrible Monday morning?"

I smile and reach for my chemistry books.

Sofia says, "It's her lab partner, Paul."

"Paul? Paul, who she's known forever? Paul, who doesn't speak English?"

"He speaks English perfectly well," I say.

"He didn't in eighth grade when we had drama together. He hung out with ESL kids."

"Yeah, well, a lot can happen in three years."

"Wow," Fen says. "I'm, like, totally shocked. A boy likes you."

I gently shove Fen out of the way. "Get over it, rugby boy."

And so I float through the day. Paul and I sit next to each other in chemistry and make shy small talk. He shows me some photos from our cloud watching and a video he made set to an EDM track. I tell him about the giant mushroom growing in my neighbor's front lawn. At lunch Sofia makes a weak excuse about having homework to do so I can walk to investor's club with Paul alone. I show him the investments I've made based on Zeyda's advice. When the bell rings for the end of lunch, I even feel brave enough for writing class.

At the end of the day Paul finds me at my locker with Sofia. She says hi and then tries to pretend she's not there.

"What are you up to now?" Paul asks.

"Usually I visit my grandfather after school on Monday."

"Oh." Paul looks disappointed.

Behind Paul, Sofia mouths *Cancel!* at me.

"I could probably visit him tomorrow instead," I say.

Paul perks up. "Really?"

"I think so." My heart is racing now. Sofia is smiling and nodding at me. "Yeah, I think that would be okay."

"Do you want to come over to my house? We could finish up that math homework."

It sounds like he really means homework. I hesitate a moment. His house. There probably won't be anyone else there. Paul's waiting for me to answer, and I wonder if maybe I should suggest the library or a coffee shop. Then Paul says, "It's not far." His easy smile makes it hard to say no.

"Okay," I say. "I'll call my grandfather on the way."

When I turn to look back at Sofia as Paul and I walk down the hall together, she gives me a big smile.

The torrential downpour has become a steady drizzle. We pull up our hoods and trudge through the puddles.

I dial Zeyda's number as we walk. The phone rings three times, and then Zeyda picks up. "Hi, Zeyda, it's Sydney."

"Are you going to be late again?" Zeyda asks. His voice sounds old and croaky, like he hasn't used it all day.

"Actually, I'm going to come tomorrow instead of today."

"Oh." Zeyda sounds disappointed, and guilt pokes me. I glance over at Paul, who is trying to walk beside me without looking like he's listening.

"I don't have my bike today because of the rain."
This is true, although I could take the bus to his house.
"Did you think about going to the JCC?" I ask, mainly to
distract myself from my guilt.

"Forget about that," Zeyda says. "I was hoping we'd
go to the casino."

"The casino? Today? How were we going to get there?"

"I thought you'd take me in my car."

"Zeyda, I don't have a full license yet."

"*Nu*, when are you going to learn? Your father told me
he drove when he was fourteen."

"That was on a farm in Manitoba, and he drove a tractor
on the weekends for a job. I don't think he had to worry
about highway traffic or parallel parking. And I *am* learning.
I still need someone who drives to be in the car with me."

"Aha," Zeyda says. "I can be in the car with you."

"I need someone with a valid license."

"Bah, there's too many rules in the world." Zeyda is
still pissed he lost his license after his stroke. His car, a
Lincoln Continental, is sitting in his garage. Mom has
offered to sell it a zillion times, but he's not interested.
"Anyway," he says, "we could take a taxi."

"All the way to Richmond? That sounds expensive.
Besides, you have to be twenty-one to get into the casino."

"You could wait for me outside."

I snort. "That doesn't sound very fun. Hey, why don't
you ask Crystal to take you? There's probably a seniors'
hour during the day."

Zeyda hesitates. "Your mother told her not to take me anymore."

"Oh."

"She's worried I'm gambling away her inheritance," Zeyda announces.

I sigh. "Okay, Zeyda, I'll see you tomorrow—at your house."

"Goodbye, Sydney."

I switch off my phone and turn to Paul. "My grandfather, my zeyda, he wanted me to take him to River Rock, the casino in Richmond."

Paul grins. "My grandmother likes to gamble too—mah jong."

"Does she live here?"

"Nah, she's in Hong Kong. I see her in the summer. Do you see your grandfather often?"

"I try to. He's pretty lonely since my grandmother died, but he's kind of hard to hang out with because he's very grumpy. My sister refuses to even talk to him."

"But you like to hang out with him?"

I nod. "Yep. I usually go a couple times a week."

Paul gives me a slow smile. "You're a different kind of person."

I feel my cheeks color. "Whaddya mean?"

"Not everyone is interested in investing or willing to hang out with their grumpy grandfather."

"True enough." I give him a sidelong glance. "Are you calling me a geek?"

Paul laughs. "No, I'm not calling you anything. I thought you'd be the kind of person who wouldn't laugh at me for sending mushroom pictures, and I was right." Paul takes my hand in his. We're holding hands. And we're having a normal conversation. I knew you could do this, I tell myself.

"Actually, the mushroom picture was pretty weird," I say. "I mean, it was a really ugly mushroom." Paul looks uncertain for a second, then pokes me in the side. "Okay, fine," I say. "It was a great picture."

When we arrive at Paul's house, I start to get nervous again. His house is tall and narrow, with a gold-colored door knocker and birds etched into frosted glass above the front door. Inside, there's cream-colored carpet and a hall table with nothing on it except an empty bowl. Paul tosses his keys in the bowl, hangs up my coat and leads me past the living room and dining room to the kitchen. I've never been in a less lived-in house. There are no discarded gym bags, no briefcases or boots in the front hall, no books or magazines lying on the coffee table in the sparsely decorated living room, no sign of the dining room ever being used. The only decorations are some Chinese calligraphy and a black-ink painting of a turtle in the living room.

The kitchen has a U-shaped counter with a breakfast bar, and sliding doors that lead to a small deck. The yard is a green square with a row of hedges beside the garage. The only ungainly thing in the kitchen is a giant shiny garbage can with a black plastic bag bursting over the lid. Beside it, takeout containers tower out of a recycling box.

"Wow, your house is so neat," I say. I want to say it looks like no one lives here, but that would sound rude. I sit on a stool at the counter.

Paul takes two glasses out of the cupboard. "It's just me here most of the time," he says.

"What do you mean?"

"My dad lives in Hong Kong, and my mom got remarried last year, and her husband works in China mostly, so she's there a lot. She's here every couple of months to see me and make sure everything's okay, read my report cards. She's coming next week."

"You live alone?" I try to keep the surprise out of my voice.

"Some of the time. My sister Julie's supposed to be 'taking care' of me. She's twenty-four, but she stays with her boyfriend, Tim, a lot."

"Wow." I look around the kitchen again. Except for the towering garbage, it looks pretty clean. "Who does stuff around the house when your mom's not here?"

"There's a cleaner and a gardener. And you know my buddy Wilson? I stay at his house most weekends and eat there. Do you want something to drink?"

I say sure, and Paul pours us each a glass of soda. "You know, that's like every kid's dream—to live alone," I say.

Paul frowns. "Yeah, it's okay. No one tells me what to do, but it's also kinda boring and lonely. Plus, if I mess up and, like, burn the place down or do crappy at school, my parents and my stepdad will totally lose it."

"Do they ever talk about sending you back to Hong Kong?"

"They talk about it, but I've been here so long, and my Chinese reading isn't that good, so I probably wouldn't do well at school. Plus, I have asthma, and the air is better here."

I look around the kitchen. The only thing on the counter is a fruit bowl with some browning bananas in it. "Who cooks for you during the week?" I can't imagine making all my own meals. I'd live on yogurt and fruit or cheese and crackers. Or I'd make a pot of squash soup and eat that every day for a week.

"Mostly me. Wilson's mom takes me grocery shopping sometimes. Julie shows up every now and then when she feels guilty and takes me out or brings me groceries. I eat a lot of takeout, but I can cook."

I nod. "Cool. What do you like to make?"

"I can make hamburgers and pasta, but mostly I eat Chinese food—stir-fries and noodle stuff. You hungry?"

"Sure."

Paul smiles and starts taking vegetables out of the refrigerator.

I watch him mince garlic and onions and throw them in a wok with some peppers and tofu. "I cheat a little," he says as he adds bottled sweet-and-sour sauce and precooked noodles from a package. "When my mom makes it from scratch, it's better." The vegetables sizzle as Paul flips them expertly with a long-handled spatula. A few minutes later he dishes the food into little bowls and hands me a pair of chopsticks. "Or would you prefer a fork?" he asks.

"Chopsticks are fine," I say.

I should feel more nervous, being alone in Paul's house with him, but I'm not. I've known Paul forever, and he knows me too.

After we eat, we go down to the basement, where there's a TV, leather couches and more cream-colored carpet. I spy a pool table through a door in an unfinished part of the basement. Paul says, "You like pool?"

I nod.

"We can play later if you want."

"Sure."

We work on the chemistry lab awhile, and when we get bored with it, we work on some math questions. For a while we concentrate, pencils scratching, Paul tapping at his calculator. I keep stealing glances at him, watching the way he tugs his hair when he's thinking through a problem. Eventually he shoves his books away, rubbing his forehead.

"You all done?" I ask.

"For now. I have time to work on it later." I think about Paul alone in the house. It's only four thirty.

"I should get going," I say.

"Wait." Paul pats the couch beside him. "Don't leave yet."

I sit back down, smooth out my pink skirt. It feels too loud now, like most of Abby's clothes. I swallow when Paul takes my hand.

My heart starts thumping in my chest. I want to hold his hand, I really do, but his other hand takes my shoulder, turning me gently toward him. If I start to break, I'll never be able to put the pieces back together. Paul is leaning forward to kiss me. I close my eyes because I don't know how to make it stop, and I don't want to either. And then Paul's mouth is on mine, moving gently. It's warm and wet, and I want him to keep going. He leans back on the couch and I do too, and then his hands are in my hair, which also feels good. I want to enjoy the kiss, but Paul's hands are snaking around to hold my back, like this is going to be more than kissing. I feel a rush of heat sweep through me, and I press myself closer to Paul even though my brain is wondering what the hell I'm doing. I've never felt this way, like I want to start unbuttoning Paul's shirt or, even crazier, my own. My breath quickens, and I start to sweat. Then I pull away, smoothing my hair. "I think I need to leave now."

"Now?" Paul rubs his hands through his hair.

"Yes, now." I finger-comb my hair and start packing up my books.

"Syd." Paul grabs my hand. "You could stay and play pool or just hang out."

"Um, maybe another time." My pulse is racing, and I want to get out.

"I didn't mean to scare—"

"It's okay." I cut him off before he says anything embarrassing. I'm backing away, stuffing my books into my bag, but I'm moving too quickly, and I can't get the zipper around my binder.

Paul leaps up from the couch and passes me my pencil case. "Are you mad at me?"

"No, no." I hide my face in my hands. "I'm glad I came, but now I need to go." I grab the rest of my stuff and rush up the stairs. Paul runs behind me, trying to keep up.

He hands me my coat at the front door while I shove my feet into my flats. "Please don't leave like this. I don't want you to think I was too..." Paul lets the sentence trail off.

"It's not you. You were good." I hesitate. "I wanted to kiss you."

Paul exhales. "Okay, good."

I shove my arms into my jacket. "But now I need to leave." I let myself out the front door without saying anything else. I can see Paul watching me from the front window, so I resist the urge to bolt down the street. I wish I had my bike. I wish I had wings. I wish I could fly away and leave my burning skin behind me. I wish I could cry a little to relieve the tension pulsing inside me.

The walk home is twenty minutes of nothing but sidewalk and drizzle and side-street traffic, enough time to try and walk away from the scene I have caused. I sweat in my rain jacket, and a blister forms on my heel from my silver flats as I try to walk everything out of my head. The rain slides off my jacket and soaks my leggings.

When I get home I pull off my sweater and sit in my tank top and leggings in the living room, flicking through channels on the TV. Then I unload the dishwasher and organize the mail Mom's left in a messy stack on the counter. I check my phone. Sofia has texted, **I saw you leave with Paul!**

I type back, **Yes.**

And?

Call me.

A minute later my phone rings. "I need details," Sofia says.

"There was kissing," I confess.

"I knew you could do it!"

I groan. "Nah, I kinda freaked out."

"Whaddya mean?"

"I had to leave."

"Did you, like, say-goodbye leave or run-away-screaming leave?"

"A bit of both. I said goodbye, I said I had to leave, but then I felt like screaming."

Sofia sighs. "That's not so bad. You can fix that."

"How?"

"Send him a text. Say thank you. Say see you tomorrow."

"That's it?"

"Yes. That's it."

"Do I have to?"

"Tomorrow will be weird if you don't."

I rub my forehead. "Okay. I'll call you back in a few minutes."

I hang up. Should I write **I had fun at your house?** That sounds ridiculous. How about **thanks for the good time?** I flop back on the couch and take a few deep breaths. What did Sofia say? I type, **See you tomorrow.**

Paul writes, **OK. Until then.**

I clutch my phone. *Until then* sounds good—romantic even.

I call Sofia. "I texted him and he wrote back."

"So you're good now?" she asks.

"I think so."

"Syd, this is so exciting!"

"I don't think I can handle it," I wail.

"No, wait," Sofia says. "You can do this. Just think of Paul as a third friend. You have me and Fenny and now Paul."

"But..."

"But what?"

I struggle to find the right words to describe the things I want to do with Paul, and how surprising this is to me. I settle on "I don't think I can make the kind of eye contact I'll need to be with Paul."

Sofia sighs. "Keep your eyes closed."

"You know what I mean."

"It'll be okay," she says softly. "Paul is a good guy— he gets you."

I want to say more to explain what's bothering me, that it's not only what Paul wants, but what I might want, only I don't know how to talk about this. It's still muddled up in my head.

Sofia and I say goodbye, and then I close my eyes and lie back on the couch.

What I want, these feelings, they may be new to me, but not to Sofia. Last year she had a thing for this guy Carlos, and she was always sighing about how "in lust" she was.

You mean in love? I would ask.

No, in lust, she insisted.

Carlos was an exchange student from Mexico in her drama class. We had to follow him around, look at his posts on social media and go places to catch glimpses of him hanging out with his friends. It was boring and occasionally embarrassing, but Sofia does lots of things for me, so I followed along. I totally didn't get why she was interested in this guy. He has the sexiest accent, she would say. Sofia also spent a lot of time obsessing over his complexion, which, I have to admit, was a really beautiful olive color.

Eventually Sofia hooked up with Carlos at a party for her drama class. She called me the next day to tell me all the gross details about what she did with him in some corner of a basement. I just knew he would have sensual hands, she moaned. Unfortunately, Carlos never had anything to do with her after that. He didn't respond to her texts or say more than hi at school. When she sent a picture of herself to him—luckily, just a head shot—she overheard some boys in her drama class snickering over it and saying porny things about her. Sofia freaked out and ended up dropping drama. She had to go to summer school and pick up another course instead of going to Croatia to visit her family with her mom. I'm so off guys, she groaned. Which isn't really true. Now she claims she's interested in *men* instead. She's got what she calls a *lust-crush* on an older guy in her building, and she is always talking to one of the young male teachers at school.

And me, am I in lust too? I shake my head as if to get rid of the thought. Then I stand up and start pacing around the room. I need a plan to cope, to visualize being successful. It's something Dr. Spenser said I could use for situations that freak me out. Okay, here goes. I am at school, and Paul and I are sitting in front of my locker, eating lunch or listening to music on his phone. We're sitting close enough that his arm is around me. I can feel his heat. Sofia is smiling and waving as she walks away from us to go to art club. Paul whispers "Until now" in my ear, and his breath is warm on my neck. Other kids are looking at us in the hall because they've never seen us together like this before, and this makes me hang my head, but it's okay because Paul kisses the back of my neck, and little shivers are running down my spine and he's squeezing my shoulder, but we're in public, so that's as far as it goes.

I open my eyes. That wasn't so bad. And I'm smiling now and more relaxed than before. I feel like calling Sofia back and telling her not to worry. Instead I text her. **Feeling better. Shy girl thinks maybe she can do this boy thing.** She sends me back a smiley face.

Then I notice Paul has sent me a picture of a cherry tree in bloom. **Beautiful,** I write back. **Take me there.**

Paul writes back, **Anytime.**

I'm feeling much better by the time Abby comes home. She storms by me, an angry look on her face, and heads down to the tent without even saying hello. I follow her downstairs and watch her throw herself onto the tent cushions.

"What's with you?" I ask.

Abby lifts her head to glare at me. "Our school is a rat hole of misogynist freaks."

"Did something happen today?"

"Yes!" Abby says emphatically, rolling her eyes.

"Are you going to tell me?"

Abby kicks a leg in the air to sit herself upright. "You won't believe it, but the school has decided our vagina play can't be part of the drama festival."

A moment of relief surges through me, so strong that I have to lean on the wall for support. I won't have to change my name or go to a different high school after all. I try to look sympathetic. "Was it your cunt monologue they had an issue with?" I can't help smirking.

Abby glares at me again. "They didn't name a specific monologue. They just said they didn't think it was appropriate for a high school audience. Have you ever heard such bullshit? How can the state of women's bodies, our safety, our health and well-being, not be *appropriate for a high school audience*? Fifty percent of the school has a vagina, including that bitch of a vice-principal."

"Did they give more details than that?"

Abby sighs. "Apparently there are religious kids at our school who would be offended by such a frank discussion of sexuality, especially the premarital kind." She sits up and rakes her hands through her hair. "What the fuck? Are we living in the 1950s? Do they think we're not having sex? Do they think girls aren't being raped at our school? Are our bodies so unspeakable, we can't talk about the parts we all have?"

I'm still hung up on her comment about kids at school having sex. Of course, I know some kids are having sex, but when I think about the details—about Abby having sex, or Sofia, or, god forbid, Fen—it feels different. Uncomfortable. I push the thought out of my mind. Everybody is having sex except me (and maybe Fen). I can barely kiss Paul. I stop and think about this. I kissed Paul. And it was good. And I want to do it again. At least, I think I do. Wait, who is Abby having sex with? She hasn't mentioned any particular guy. Abby only talks about girls. I turn to Abby, who is still waving her hands and going on about the stupid vice-principal. Is Abby having sex with girls? Wait, I don't want to imagine Abby with anyone, male or female. Unfortunately, a picture of Abby making out with her friend Sunita takes over my mind. I push it away, but it comes back again. Sunita has been at our house a lot—and in the tent a lot.

Abby declares, "You know what I'm going to do? I'm going to plaster this all over social media. I mean, right now. There are feminist organizations that are going to freak when they hear this. And the mainstream media—they need to know too." Abby stands up and heads toward her room.

"Where are you going?"

"I have work to do," Abby calls without looking back.

I head upstairs to start dinner without Abby—a fish stir-fry with slivered almonds. I cut up the broccoli and the other vegetables, make the sauce and start the rice.

By the time we eat, Abby is like a phoenix newly risen. She has shaken off her anger and frustration and moved on to pure passion. Throughout dinner she describes her complete action plan—her social-media strategy, the videos she's going to make, the song she wants to write, the protest dance she and her fellow "cuntsters" will perform. I keep hoping Mom and Dad will tell her it's only a play or suggest that perhaps they should do *High School Musical* instead. They seem just as amused as when I asked if I could invest my university fund with Zeyda, which pisses me off. Clearly, my investment plans should have been taken more seriously than Abby's silly play. Perhaps it would have been better if Abby had put on the play at school after all. It would have been one day of torture, and perhaps I could have been sick that day. I could have run away for twenty-four hours until Abby's freak show of a sex play was over. Now it's going to be a whole social-media campaign, a protest march with a candlelight "vagil." Perhaps I'll have to go live with Zeyda and attend some west-side high school. Or maybe I'll just hide out at Sofia's for a while.

Mom and Dad clean the kitchen, since I cooked. In the basement I find Abby typing away on her laptop at the desk in the rec room. "More 'vagil' planning?" I ask.

"No, I'm in guerrilla theater mode now."

"What's that?"

"We're going to put on the play anyway."

I grip the wall. "Even though the school said no?"

"Yep."

"How much trouble will you be in then?"

Abby grins. "It'll be the ultimate protest."

"How are you going to sneak a whole play onstage in the middle of the festival?"

Abby cocks her head. "I think it'll have to be on during school, maybe lunch hour. We won't tell anyone until the day of."

I exhale noisily. "If I was planning to do that, I wouldn't sleep until the play was over."

"It *is* exciting." Abby grins. "I think we'll do it before the festival. Maybe if we raise enough of a stink, we'll get to be in the festival after all."

"That's not what I was thinking."

Abby looks back at her screen. "Yeah yeah. I know it's not your thing. But scaredy-cats don't get shit done."

I feel myself bristle. It's not that I'm scared; it's more about being embarrassed. Do we really have to talk about girl parts in public? "You know"—I tap my nails on the wall to get Abby's attention—"if you took out the words *cunt* and *vagina*, the school would probably be okay with the play. You could call it *The Girl Monologues* and talk about birth control and menstruation but leave out all the stuff about body parts."

Abby spins around in her swivel chair. "Are you serious?"

"Yes, I am. People are uncomfortable with those words. Think about health class, about tampon commercials, about any public discussion about women's bodies. You can discuss women's health without making people uncomfortable."

"Getting people to say *vagina*"—she draws out the word to make me squirm—"is the whole point. It's like women's bodies, the actual parts, are too shameful to even discuss. And if we can get over that shame, maybe we can have a real discussion about what women need."

I shake my head.

Abby groans in frustration and pushes past me into her room. "I have to call Sunita."

Sunita. I think about the noises I heard the other day, the giggling. I almost ask Abby about Sunita, but she's already closed the door to her room.

Seven

A LOW MIST HANGS OVER the city on Tuesday morning, threatening rain. I lie in bed and take stock of how I feel. Not quite as elated as yesterday, but still good. An upswing, I think. I still sense the fog, but it's at the corner of my eye. When I turn my head to look at it, it moves farther away. And there's no need to chase it. It's the kind of fog that will burn off once I get moving. Yes, a definite upswing. I decide to wear leggings, my brown boots and a long beige sweater, nothing too colorful, but not drab either. I pack some biking clothes to wear after school.

When I get to school, Paul is already in chem class, sitting at our usual spot. A smile spreads across my cheeks when I see him, and I want to hide my face because I must look ridiculous. I try hard to keep eye contact, but when I get close enough to sit down, I have to look away. I focus hard on getting out my books.

Paul wraps one arm around my shoulder and whispers in my ear, "I wanted to say sorry about yesterday."

There are only a few other students in the room, but still my cheeks heat up. I lean into him and whisper, "You don't need to say sorry."

"Are you sure?"

"Yes, I'm sure."

Paul exhales and pulls away from me. "I feel better now." He runs his hands through his hair. "Do you want to go see the cherry tree today? It's not far."

"I need to go see my grandfather. I didn't go yesterday."

"Oh, right."

"Maybe tomorrow?" I say.

Paul breaks into his smile. "Yeah, that would be good. Something to look forward to."

I smile shyly. "Okay."

The chem teacher and the other kids start coming into the room, so we move apart. I want to wipe the silly smile off my face, but I can't. Paul tousles my hair and then squeezes my hand below the table. I squeeze back until class starts.

At lunch Paul comes by my locker and sits down next to me. And it's just the way I imagined. Sofia leaves for art club. Fen is at a rugby meeting. Except I don't know what to say to Paul, and he seems equally tongue-tied. "I play soccer Wednesday nights," he tells me.

"Cool," I say.

We endure another awkward pause. Then Paul pulls out his phone. "Let me play you this song." We share his earbuds, and Paul plays me a dance mix. We're sitting close enough to touch, and Paul reaches for my hand. I grasp it—too hard, probably. I keep my head down because I'm sure people are staring at us and because I'm breathing quicker and louder than I usually do, and I don't want Paul to hear and wonder what's up with me. I want to enjoy sitting here with him, but I also feel like drumming my fingers on my lunch bag, on my math binder, anything to relieve my anxiety, and that makes me frustrated. When the song ends, I stand up.

"I have some other homework I need to do now, for my writing class." It's true. I haven't made any headway on my poetry assignment.

Paul stands up. "Are you going to send me something you've written one day?"

"Maybe." My toes are tapping anxiously.

"I'll see you tomorrow?"

"Yeah, sure." I nod.

I watch Paul saunter off, one earbud still in his ear, and feel a mixture of relief and disappointment. As soon as he's out of sight, I pull on my jacket and head out to the big willow trees at the edge of the field. The mist has turned into a light rain. I pull out my phone and play some rapid-fire Sudoku to quell my nerves until the bell rings. Then I force myself to get up and go to writing class.

I'm glad I promised to visit Zeyda after school. I change into my bike clothes and get out of school quickly so that I'll have time to bike past Zeyda's house and chug up the hill to UBC and then coast back down. Being on my bike feels good, to sense only my heaving lungs and aching quads as I grind up the steep hill, the ocean glinting through the trees. At the top of the hill I do a quick loop through the campus and then surge down the hill, the wind rushing past my ears. I arrive at Zeyda's damp from rain and sweat and drained of the nervous energy that has dogged me all day.

Crystal lets me in, pours me a large glass of water and tells me Zeyda's outside on the balcony. I pull open the heavy sliding door and find Zeyda wrapped in a blanket, staring out at the sea from a deck chair. From the balcony you can usually see the downtown skyline and the mountains. Today everything is swathed in low fog, just the mountain peaks poking through the clouds, barely visible against the whiteness of the sky.

Zeyda looks up at my sweaty head. "Did you run a marathon to get here?"

"No, I just biked up to UBC and back."

"For fun?"

"Yes."

Zeyda shakes his head. "*Meshugganah*"—crazy— he mumbles.

"It's fun," I say. My phone pings, and I pull it out of my bike bag. Paul has written, **I looked for you after school.**

At my gf's, I write back.

Can I call you later?

I send a smiley face.

"Is that boy writing you again?" Zeyda asks.

"Yes," I say. "You can call him Paul, not *that boy*."

"The one that's not Jewish."

"Yes, Zeyda." I sigh, sitting down in a deck chair next to him. "I'm putting my phone away, and Paul's not going to text me anymore. I'm here to see you." I pat his knee. "How's the shipping industry today? Any cruise ships out?"

"He's your boyfriend?" Zeyda asks.

I shrug. "Not sure." It's too complicated to explain to Zeyda.

Zeyda cocks his head to the side. "What do you mean? Either he is or he isn't."

"It's too early to define things. We're friends."

"Friends today, but tomorrow he'll be your boyfriend, and poof, there goes the Jewish people."

I roll my eyes and flop back in my chair.

"Paul and I are just friends, and even if we were—" I struggle for the right word. Dating? Going out? "—more than friends, it doesn't mean we're getting married or anything."

Zeyda shakes his finger at me. "Look at what happened to your mother's friend's daughter, that Rachel.

They were only friends to start. Your generation is ruining Judaism."

Zeyda's referring to Mom's friend Miri's daughter, who married a non-Jewish guy, Carter, last year.

I roll my eyes again, and Zeyda asks me, "Your parents know about this non-Jewish boy?"

"No, but not because he's not Jewish. Because he's, well, he's a boy. And he's not really my boyfriend. And it's private." I look down at my shoes.

"Oh." Zeyda smiles and pats my hand. "Then I won't say anything."

That's just like Zeyda, to get fired up about something, but then understand when he's crossed a line, when I need his help. "Let's talk about something else," he says.

I nod. "Yes. I didn't come to argue with you."

"Fine. Let's play a game."

"Checkers?"

Zeyda nods again. "I bet you five dollars I can beat you."

"You're on."

I get the game from the cupboard, and we play three games. Zeyda wins the first two, but I win the last game, so I only owe him five dollars. When I try to pay him, he pushes my money away. "You'll win it back next time," he says.

I kiss him on the top of his head and bike home. The sun has come out, as if to remind the city it still exists, and it lingers along the horizon. At least the days are getting longer, the rainiest part of the year almost over. I feel the fog less in the summer.

Usually the stop-and-go nature of biking in the city— the endless traffic lights, the slow-moving vehicles, the need to worry about car doors being flung open in front of me—frustrates me, but tonight I'm thinking about what would happen if I went back to Paul's house, back to that couch in the basement, back to lying next to him. I press against my bike seat and almost sail through an intersection. While I wait for the light to change, I force myself back to reality. I spend the rest of the ride home focusing on the traffic.

When I get home Mom is in the kitchen, making hamburgers and corn on the cob. "Isn't Dad supposed to cook tonight?" I ask.

"He's volunteering at the hospice tonight, so I said I would do his dinner."

I raise my eyebrows. "I still don't get what he's doing with sick people."

"I think it's nice," Mom says, her hands in the raw hamburger.

I slump into a chair to check my phone. Paul has texted, **How was your grandfather?**

Crazy, I write back.

"How was school?" Mom asks.

"Fine," I say, not looking up.

Why crazy? Paul asks.

I'll have to tell you in person, I type back.

Want to come over?

Sorry, family dinner. Maybe tomorrow. I could go see Paul after dinner, but after being with Zeyda and then biking home, I want to sit quietly. And I can't deal with all the excitement of Paul. I still need to think about how to be with him. That could take forever.

"Who are you texting?" Mom asks.

"Just my lab partner, Paul."

I glance at Mom to see if she'll ask anything about Paul, but all she says is "Did you see Zeyda today?"

"Yes, he was grumpy and extra crazy."

"What else is new? Is he still refusing to come to the Seder?"

"We didn't even get to that."

"Maybe we'll kidnap him and bring him here."

"He'd be miserable and ruin it for you." I drift out of the kitchen and head downstairs. From the doorway of my room I see the closet waiting for me, the door slightly open. You don't need to go in there, I tell myself. It's just a habit. And there's no fog today—at least, not much. Still, I feel like sitting in the closet, hiding out from the world for a bit. I won't though. That's for desperate times. Instead, I go into the tent in the other room, lie down and close my eyes.

After dinner I'm hoping to hang out and do some home-work in front of the TV, but Mom's invited her Jewish music group over to practice Passover songs. The entire upstairs vibrates with competing guitars and jangling tambourines. Someone's even brought a bongo. Then Abby troops down-stairs with Sunita and three other girls I recognize from school.

"Oh," Abby says when she sees me in the tent. "We were going to rehearse here tonight."

I look up at the girls clutching their bags and their scripts. Great. Now the vagina monologues aren't only at my school—they're at my house. I get up and go into my room and try to focus on my poetry assignment.

Upstairs, someone's tapping their feet vigorously, making my light fixture jiggle. From across the hall I hear Sunita and Abby laughing loudly. I pick up my pen and scribble in my journal, *I need a new space, a new place without the music and vagina talk. Place, space, race, your face, makes me turn into a head case, I'm such a waste.*

I could call Paul and go to his house, and we could work or watch TV. It would be okay if I called him, but I haven't figured out what to do about being with him, and I'm too exhausted to talk about that. *Fear, your ear, the sweet edge of it, warm and pulsing, so near.* I'll never be able to hand in any of these lines for class. *Paul* rhymes with *tall*, but it also rhymes with *wall* and *fall*. What is a poem anyway?

Maybe tomorrow I'll go back to Paul's. We could make dinner together and play pool in the basement. And then we'd kiss again, and his hands would be in my hair, on my skin. We might be on that leather couch in the basement. I feel my face flush thinking about it. And then what, we're naked on the couch? I open my eyes and grab my hair. I can't even think about kissing Paul, let alone... I am ridiculous, and I hate myself. *Hate is my fate, second rate, take cover from being a lover, never are you to be loved.*

I hear giggling from the other room. I slam my writing book closed and sit on the basement stairs by the open door to the rec room, listening.

"Well, I'm working on my cunt monologue," Abby says.

"And we have Jay's monologue about wanting a vagina," one of Abby's friends, Emma, adds.

"We need to ask him," Abby says, "if he still wants to be in it even though it's not part of the festival."

"I think we should agree to call him *she*," Emma says.

"Oh, is that what...she wants?" Sunita asks.

"Yes," Emma says.

"Fine. We'll ask Jay if she wants to perform her monologue," Abby says.

Abby and her friends continue organizing their monologues. One of the girls is going to perform a monologue about consent, and Emma wants to talk about periods and the ridiculousness of tampon ads. "Can you

imagine," she says, "if there was actually an ad with a girl
having cramps and feeling horrible?"

"You should create a mock ad for Advil of a girl with a
heating pad shoved down her pants," Sunita says.

"Yes!" Abby says. "I love it! We could have a chorus of
tampons in the background, barbershop style, singing a
menstrual doo-wop."

I bury my head in my hands.

Then Abby says, "Let's make sure the performance
isn't too heavy overall, that it's not only the gloom and
doom of sexuality. This has to be about the glory of
vaginas, about what a woman's body can do."

I wince as the girls giggle.

"My monologue is going to be about girl lust," Sunita
says. "That should balance it out."

I wince again.

Only Abby has finished her monologue, so she reads
it to the other girls. I know I should run away and not
listen, but I'm too curious. It's the kind of curiosity I wish
I didn't have, like watching a movie where you know
there'll be a train wreck and you know you should turn
away, but you can't.

Abby begins reading: "My grandmother could never
say the word *vagina*. Instead she called her girl parts a
knish, which is a Jewish word for a potato-stuffed pastry.
It's a yummy thing to eat, and I think my grandmother
must have had a positive vision of her body, even if she
couldn't say the word *vagina*."

OMG. I want to shove my fingers in my ears or walk away, but I don't. I pull a pillow over my head to muffle the sound.

Abby continues, "I have issues with the word *vagina* too, so I almost never say it. I thought it was because I didn't like the sound of the *v*, the awkward *g*. Instead I call girl parts *hoo-haw* or *froo-froo*, but those are baby words that belittle women's bodies. Mostly I say *girl parts*.

"Boys and men have lots of awful words for vaginas, like *twat* and *hole*. There are tons of other awful words on the Internet. I don't know why you would demean something so amazing, something that gave you life, with those words.

"Some people are resolved to call it what it is and shudder their way through *vagina*, the proper word, but that's not good enough for me either. *Vagina* is only part of the parts, not the whole deal, and if you were to look up the meaning of the word, you'd find it means 'scabbard.' What's that, you say? Well, it's a sheath for a knife, and if you ask me, I don't have a vagina, if that's what it means. Girl parts are so much more.

"Do we have a word for the whole thing, all the girl parts together? We do. It's called a *cunt*. Now stay with me. I know you're thinking, Isn't that dirty? Isn't that the worst word you can think of? Isn't that a swearword you rarely hear used? It hasn't made it to radio or casual swearing. Not like *fuck* or *shit*."

I cringe when Abby says the c-word. How long is this monologue anyway? Abby goes on.

"*Cunt* may be a swearword now, a curse, but it wasn't always so. In many languages, from Irish to Chinese, from Arabic to Latin, *cunt* was a word for witches, priestesses, for women and for goddesses. *Cunt* was a word of praise. In many Middle Eastern and African languages, *cunta* meant 'woman.' It is only now that it means negative things, like 'whore' and 'bitch' or worse. It is only now that we hate our bodies so much that our most private girl parts, which used to be holy, are called by the worst word we know. I say let's reclaim the word for our bodies. Let's make *cunt* sacred again. Let's protect, love and treasure women's bodies. Let's use a word for women's parts that will shield us from rape, from gender mutilation, from shame. Let's use a word for our bodies that celebrates their power. I don't have only a *vagina*, I have a *cunt*."

Abby finishes and the other girls pause, letting the words sink in, and then they clap. I let myself collapse back on the stairs. Good god. She's going to say that at school? In front of an audience? With teachers present? Even listening to her in the basement of my own house is too much. I'll have to be sick that day. I stumble back to my room, close the door and turn on some music to drown out any more girl-parts talk or the sound of Mom's music group thumping out "Dayenu" with tambourines.

And if I was going to write a vagina monologue? Well, I wouldn't. But if I did, it would be called "My Cunt Is Sleeping." I take out my journal and scribble, *My cunt isn't talking to you right now because it's not interested, thank you very much. It doesn't even like to make eye contact. It's a non-contact cunt. Except I wouldn't call it a cunt or a vagina or anything else. It's like Voldemort, the Place That Cannot Even Be Named.*

I slam my journal shut and lie back on the bed with my fingers jammed in my ears. I try to think about Paul—his smile, the way he tugs on my hand or gets excited about clouds and mushrooms. I like how he scratches his head with his pencil when he's thinking about a quadratic equation.

And I like how he kissed me.

But I'm the girl who's too freaked out to kiss him back.

Eight

I WAKE UP EARLY THE NEXT MORNING before it's light out, as if my body is giving me an extra hour to convince myself to get up. I'm bored with Sudoku, so I do KenKen, and then I try a crossword, but I suck at it. Numbers are easier than words, more reliable. I recite square roots as high as I can. When the light starts to creep around the blinds, I get out of bed and shower. *Fog, I will ignore you, tell you to fuck off. Fuck off, fog.* I rub at my head. I wash my hair and then straighten it and add little braids at the front for something to do. I spend a long time trying to decide what to wear, pulling out half the clothes in my closet and trying on three different outfits before settling on jeans, silver flats and a gray polka-dot shirt. It's still early, only 6:30 AM. I take out my journal and jot down a few early-morning words: *fog, stuck in a bog, a heavy weight that can't wait, darkness*

*pressing me down, until I'm so thin you can drive over me.
Paul, come and puff me up, until I'm floating.*

All of this sucks.

I go upstairs and make scones for everyone's breakfast,
filling the house with the smell of blueberries and corn-
meal. At least everyone else will wake up in a good mood.

The fog burns off as I make my way through the day, as
the sun starts to slant through the sky. By the time I get
to writing class, I feel like I can handle life, like I might
make it to the weekend. Then Mrs. Lee has us do a free-
write called "I Fear."

"Write about what scares you most," she says. "Don't
edit as you go along or judge what you've written.
Keep your pen moving, and if you go off on a memory or
a tangent, keep writing."

Everyone pulls out paper and pens or starts tapping
away on personal devices. I pull out my journal and feel
the fog rise higher in my head. What am I scared of?
Where to start?

I write, *I'm scared of this class and what might happen
when we hand in assignments, and I'm very scared of Paul and
talking to him. I'm scared of him liking me and me liking him
back. I'm scared of talking to him and maybe doing other things,
and even thinking about those things scares me. I'm scared
Sofia might say something to him and screw everything up.*

I'm scared he's going to touch me and I'll fall apart. I chew on the end of my pen for a moment now that I've got that all written down. *I'm scared of crashing on my bike and losing all my teeth. I'm scared of the ocean coming up onto Zeyda's house if there's a tsunami and I'm scared he'll get senile and I won't want to visit him anymore. Then Crystal will quit and he'll have to go to a home and he won't ever talk to me again. I'm scared of losing Zeyda's money on the stock market, and I'm scared of grade twelve and everything after that.*

I stop to take a breath and shake out my hand. I want the time to be up, for Mrs. Lee to say, "Okay, everyone, stop," but she doesn't, so I start writing again. *I'm scared the fog will be so big and so heavy that I won't be able to get up. Mom will come down, and I'll look so pathetic, and she'll say, "C'mon, Syd," but I won't be able to move. I'm scared to think about what would happen next.* I stop, even though Mrs. Lee hasn't told us to. There it is, the fog, written down on paper. I feel exhausted. Then I scratch out the last paragraph until the paper rips, and I'm so busy doing that, I don't even notice the time's up and people have stopped writing. Mrs. Lee is saying, "Now write what you aren't scared of. Write about the things you know you can do."

I take a deep breath. This is easier, safer. *I'm not scared of monsters or wild dogs or coyotes or steep hills. I'm not scared of failing math or chem. I'm not scared of going to university or dark lanes or ogres, fairies or beasts. I'm not scared of riding my bike or Abby or even her play. Embarrassed, yes, but not scared.*

Mrs. Lee says we should start thinking about our poetry portfolios and continue to read the poems she's assigned for the course. She says to reread our in-class writing to start a poem. I glance back through my writing. I pray no poems come out of these fears. By the time class ends I feel like I need to lie down instead of heading to Mandarin.

I stop in the bathroom and duck into a stall, my journal like contraband under my arm. I can't leave those words lurking in my handwriting, so I grab the pages and rip them out of the book. Half the pages get stuck in the tightly sewn binding, leaving an ugly ruffle of paper. I want to find scissors and cut the ruffle out, make my book tidy again, but scissors won't fix the mess. I hesitate in the stall. I'd planned to rip the pages into little pieces and flush them down the toilet, but the bell rings and I have to get going, so I stick the pages back in the book and shove the journal between the pages of my Mandarin workbook. It feels like I'm carrying a bomb that might detonate at any moment, so I make a detour to my locker and drop the journal in my backpack, even though it makes me late for class.

After school Paul is waiting for me by my locker, as if it's a normal thing for him to do. I can't resist smiling at him, even though I'm exhausted from writing class and stressed from a pop quiz we had in Mandarin.

"Do you want to come over and play pool?" Paul asks. Even though no one around us is paying attention, I still feel like ducking my head. I could suggest the mall or Starbucks or even the trees he sent the picture of, but I also want to go back to his house. If we can be alone, without anyone else's eyes on us, that will be a relief. We can go to Paul's house and sit on the floor with our backs against the front door, limp with relief at the privacy. I can't seem to imagine anything beyond that. I nod yes, and Paul and I walk to his house. Once we're away from school, I relax a little bit. Paul takes my hand and we talk about the investor's club, about an upcoming science test.

At Paul's house the kitchen is cleaner than it was before. The garbage and recycling have been taken out; the fruit bowl is full. When Paul opens the refrigerator, I see the shelves have been restocked. "Did your sister move back in or something?" I ask.

"My mom is coming next week," Paul says, taking a bag of nuts out of a cupboard. "So Julie's been here more." He grins. "We're preparing for the inspection."

"Are you happy about your mom coming?" I ask.

"Yeah, mainly. She'll want to hear about what I'm up to, check my tests"—he riffles through a pile of mail on the counter—"and see what I'm reading. She'll also cook for me, buy me some new stuff. That part's all good. And she's good company. But she'll also lecture me about commerce programs, about university."

"That part isn't good?"

Paul shakes his head and eats a handful of nuts. "Not good."

"We could do commerce together," I say shyly.

"Is that what you want to do?"

I nod.

Paul frowns. "That's not what I want to study."

"But you're interested in the investor's club."

Paul looks down. It's the first time I've ever seen him embarrassed. "I knew you'd be there..."

Heat climbs my face. There's an awkward silence between us. Finally Paul says, "I've always known I want to study science."

"And your mom, does she like cloud watching?"

Paul laughs. "Uh, not really."

"I see."

Paul says, "My mom's okay. She's not into nature stuff, but she's always happy when I take her new places. I took her out to Bowen Island last year, mainly for the ferry ride, and she loved that. Mostly she likes going up to Queen Elizabeth Park, especially on a Sunday in the summer. She likes the view, and she likes to see the brides getting their pictures taken."

"What about your dad?"

Paul's forehead creases. "I wouldn't even mention that I'm planning on studying science to him. He thinks I'm going to go into business with him."

"What will you do about school?" I nibble on a cashew.

"I haven't figured that out yet."

I nod.

"Do your parents care what you study?" he asks.

"They just want me and Abby to follow our interests. My sister will do something in the arts." I think about Abby's play and shudder a little.

We talk for a few more minutes and eat the nuts. Paul lays one hand over mine and I lace my fingers through his, and we smile at each other, that stupid smile people do when they're, you know, in love.

Downstairs, Paul leads me past the carpeted room with the couch and TV and into an unfinished room with concrete floors and a washer and dryer and laundry sink along the outside wall. Shelves hold neat stacks of luggage and sporting equipment—skis and skates, tennis rackets and golf clubs. In the middle of the room is the pool table.

"You know how to play?" Paul says.

"I know the basics," I say. Auntie Karen and Uncle Mark have a table, and Abby and I have spent many Friday nights after dinner playing with my cousins.

Paul hands me a cue and then uses the triangle to rack up the balls. He leans over the table, takes aim and sends the balls spinning. He sinks a striped ball into a pocket. "Okay," he says, "you're solids."

I miss my targeted ball on my first shot, but then, as I start to concentrate, I sink balls with ease on my second and third turns. I relax as I focus on the game instead of on being with Paul. I almost win, but then I scratch the eight ball, and the game ends.

"Oh," Paul says, "you were doing so well."

I shrug. "Play again?"

"Sure," he says. He racks up the balls but gestures for me to take the break. I aim the cue ball carefully, and the balls ricochet across the table. Pool is mainly geometry and fine motor skills.

We take a few more turns. This is good, I think. Paul and me. We can play pool and wander around the city looking at weird stuff, like mushrooms. "Hey, where was the tree you sent me the picture of?" I ask.

Paul takes his shot and misses. "It's in VanDusen Garden."

"Off Oak Street?"

"Yeah. Have you ever been?"

I shake my head.

Paul leans against his pool cue. "My sister and I used to jump the fence to play there."

"What's there?"

"All sorts of flowers and trees and a big meadow. There's also one of those mazes made out of hedges. For a long time I couldn't see over the top."

I lean over the table and easily sink my three ball. "I remember you back then."

"Yeah?"

"You were really short in eighth grade."

Paul takes a shot. "And shy."

"I didn't think that. I just thought you didn't know English."

"Well, that was a problem too."

I focus on lining up my turn. "You couldn't have been shyer than me."

Paul smiles. "Maybe not. I remember seeing you in eighth grade for the first time."

"You do?"

"Sure. I remember thinking you were the cutest girl in the room. That's why I sat next to you."

"That's nice of you to say, but it can't be true." I aim for the seven ball and sink Paul's number one instead.

"Thanks," Paul says, pointing to the sunk ball. "It is true. I probably should have sat next to some of the other ESL kids the way I did in all my other classes, so they could help me understand. But I wanted to sit next to you." Paul steps closer to me, so we're standing face-to-face. He strokes my hair away from my cheek. I take a deep breath. "I still think you're the cutest girl in chem."

I bury my burning face in my hands. "I'm sorry," I say.

"For what?" Paul whispers into my hair.

"I don't know," I mumble. "For not even being able to look at you."

"That's okay. You don't have to look at me." His hands are still in my hair, sweeping it back from my face, then stroking my cheek. I let my hands fall from my face, and Paul strokes the back of my neck, the curve of my earlobe, sending goose bumps down my arms. We stay like that for a moment, Paul slowly moving closer to me, until he tips my face up to him and kisses me softly. "You don't even have to look at me to do this."

It's true—my eyes are closed—but I can feel Paul close to me, close enough that our chests are almost touching. I inhale to keep myself together, so that I don't crumble, and I smell the mix of his cologne or aftershave and the scent of his skin. Paul steps closer to me. His body rests against mine, our legs touching, my breasts against his chest. Paul's arms slide down my back to rest around my waist, and I hear a sigh escape out of me, louder than I want. My knees feel like they might give way, and I'll collapse into Paul's arms. I want to press myself closer, but I step away. "I'm sorry—"

"I thought—"

Paul and I smooth out our clothes. "Look, you're smart and you read social cues right," I say, "but I get freaked out by people." I step away from Paul until my back is against the laundry sink.

"By people?"

"Yes. People freak me out, and then I need to be by myself. That's why I have exactly two friends, Fen and Sofia."

"And me."

"Okay, fine—three friends. And you're, like, my new best friend, but I'm not sure I can handle that."

Paul smiles. "Your new best friend?"

"You don't have to call it that," I mumble.

He laughs. "No, I like it. I never thought of it that way." He moves close to me, so close we're almost touching again. I have to will myself not to bolt. "I like being your new best friend, and I don't want to scare you," he says evenly.

I'm sweating now, and I can feel tears burning in my eyes. "I want to be here with you, but..." I say.

"I think I sort of get it," Paul says.

We stand like that a lot longer, and it's painful. I can hear Paul's labored breathing, the effort not to touch me coiled between us. I keep my eyes down to avoid looking at him. I want to wrap my arms around him and hold him to me so tightly, yet I can't, and that pisses me off. Does that mean I'll always be alone? I feel multiplication tables forming in my head. I don't want to recite those now. I don't do that anymore. "Can we try this again?" I say.

I mean another day or maybe another lifetime, but I haven't been clear, and Paul thinks I mean now, this moment. His arms come up, and he wraps them tightly around me, pressing his hands against my back. I feel parts of him against me that I don't even want to know about. He's kissing my ear lightly, running his tongue along the lobe, and then his lips are moving along my jawline. I know I'm standing like a board in his arms, but at least I'm not pushing him away. His lips find mine and we're kissing again, and it goes on for such a long time that I almost forget to be freaked out. I wrap my hands around him and hold him. If I keep doing this, I might get to be just a body with my heart racing and my breath picking up speed. I want to be ready for that, but I'm not, and the panicky feeling comes back. I break away from Paul. "I have to go," I say. "I can't stay."

Paul lets me step away from him. "Will you come back?" he asks.

It's not a simple question. He's not only asking for homework help; he's asking for me. I think back to Zeyda telling me a nice boy sends flowers, and I wish that this was all there was to it. Paul would send me flowers, and we'd go to the movies.

"Will you come back?" Paul asks again.

"I think I have to," I say, but there's no joy in my voice. Something has been started, and I don't know how to finish it.

Then I feel really freaked out, so I back away from Paul and fix my hair. "I have to get going because I have this assignment due for my writing class soon and—"

"It's okay, Syd. I understand."

I'm not sure what he understands, but I lower my head and say, "I'll text you later."

"Okay, I'll text you back." He reaches for my hand, but I pretend not to see it—I can't start all that again. Paul lets me race up the stairs and retrieve my coat, bag and shoes by myself. Then I'm out on the street, and I want to laugh and cry. I feel like I'm drowning in something, I'm not sure what. Love and something else. Something I guess you'd call desire or craving. Those words make me cringe. I settle on the word *crave*. It's abstract enough that it doesn't make me want to crawl into a hole. People crave all kinds of things—new phones, ice cream, cigarettes. Still, I know what kind of craving I'm talking about. But how does that work if you're the kind of person who doesn't normally talk to people?

I take a deep breath and try to clear my mind. Paul is my lab partner. Paul and I do math homework together. He also has beautiful skin that I'd like to inhale. I imagine my hands traveling the length of his back, then wrapping around his narrow hips, inhaling the scent below his ear. My face burns, and I spin around in a circle as if to chase these thoughts from my head. Then I sit down on the curb and open up my journal. I write, *These cravings or desire I feel, no one ever talks about girls having them.*

I shudder, put away my journal and start walking really fast.

Being with Paul has opened up something in me, something I didn't know I had, that I don't know how to experience. I think it involves letting go. There's no way I can let the neatly ordered and controlled world I've created be blown apart by these feelings. I've never envisioned letting my body take over.

I start running because I'm not sure what to do with all the thoughts in my head. I want them to go away. I jog toward home until I'm out of breath. Then I stop and pant beside a tree. A few tears come to my eyes, and it feels good to let them run down my face. Am I scared to be happy? Or am I scared that it might not last? Paul might lift the fog now, but for how long? And what if I can't be close to him? Even thinking about it makes a tinge of fog settle on me. I shake my head to free myself. I think about Paul, about his mouth on mine, about the way we talked on the way home. I want to head back to his house and curl up on his couch and watch Netflix, but we wouldn't just watch Netflix. I think about his mouth again. The fog lifts, but a new feeling—nervousness mixed with something else—crawls up my skin. I start running again. Eventually I settle for a quick walk, and by the time I get home I'm a sweaty, exhausted mess.

I take a quick shower, focus on some Sudoku, three games to be exact, finish the math homework, make a few trades and call Zeyda. I take out my journal and reread the line I wrote earlier about girls' desire. I add, *We never talk about girls' cravings in sex-ed class. We only talk about how dangerous sex can be, the infections and unwanted pregnancies. What if the most dangerous thing about sex is that you'll want to do it? Everyone knows boys feel these ways, but for girls, we only talk about periods and girls' inside bits. What if we talked about why people want to have sex? That would be crazy and horribly embarrassing. What if the teacher focused not only on the inside parts of girls, but the outside parts too?*

I lie flat on my back on the floor with my eyes closed, trying not to think about any of my girl parts. The fog is rising like a darkness coming up from the floor and seeping into my bones. I feel it covering my skin, slowly making its way into my head. It's not only at the corner of my eyes, but in front of and behind me. I try to shove it away, but my hand moves through it. I try to get the light-bulb inside me burning so brightly it will destroy the fog, but it doesn't work. I give up. I crawl over to the closet and collapse in a corner.

I take deep breaths, trying to calm myself down, and then I imagine I'm biking with Fen somewhere flat and dry, like the prairies. I manage to keep myself calm until I hear my phone ping. I open the closet door and grab my phone off my bed. Paul texts, **Shy girl, next time we'll go see the trees.**

Okay. I pause a moment and then write, **I'm sorry I had to leave.**

It's okay.

You probably don't understand.

I don't have to understand.

I want to see you again.

Me too!

I am generally freaked out about everything.

Even me?

Yes, you.

Why?

Too complicated to talk about.

Okay.

There's a long pause. Then I type, **I don't want you to think I'm a tease.**

You are a terrible tease. He adds a smiling emoji.

I don't know what to say to that.

You don't have to say anything.

Okay. I think I have to go now.

G-bye.

My heart is racing. I think I'm in love, and I also think it's going to kill me.

By dinnertime the fog is so thick I'm sure other people can see it. When I look in the mirror, I'm convinced I can see a halo of darkness surrounding me, like I've grown a permanent shadow. I take a series of selfies from different angles and with different lighting to make sure I'm not going crazy, but it doesn't show in the photos. I try to distract myself by looking at the investing website to check my portfolio. Sofia and I are leading the contest, but I'm not that interested in our standings.

When I go upstairs for dinner, Mom's excited because the Haggadahs she ordered have come in the mail, *and* there's a complimentary CD. She's got "Go Down, Moses" blasting through the speakers attached to her laptop. Mom and Abby sing along loudly as they set the table and dish out the food. Even Dad's humming as he pours water into glasses. I want to stuff earplugs in my ears and hide in the basement.

It's Abby's night to cook, and because she thinks we should eat more vegetarian food and make a smaller imprint on the earth, she's made chickpea patties with chutney, curried potatoes and a green salad.

"I wonder if chickpeas are actually more environmentally friendly than meat," I say. "They don't grow locally, so they have to be trucked to us, and then there's the cans. Even if they can be recycled, that takes resources."

"No animals were killed for this dinner," Abby says.

I snort. "What about the rabbits who were squashed by tractors for your factory-farmed salad? Do they not count?"

"No animals were intentionally killed for this dinner. And the potatoes are organic." Then she pauses, narrows her eyes. "You are really mean."

She's right. I slink out of the kitchen to wash my hands. My fog shadow trails behind me like a bridal train.

I'm not that hungry, and I pick at my food. After dinner Dad suggests we practice driving. He needs to go to Zeyda's house and fix a window Crystal says is leaking, and I can have a quick visit.

"Oh, sure," Abby says, "you're willing to drive and put more CO_2 in the atmosphere. That's good for the environment."

"Competing to see who's killing the planet faster is a game no one can win," I shoot back.

Dad puts a hand on my shoulder and bustles me out to his Volvo before Abby can say anything else.

"We should get a Prius," I say.

Dad tosses me the keys. "Just learn to drive so Zeyda will agree to go somewhere with you."

"Is that what this is about? I get to be Zeyda's chauffeur?"

Dad grins. "Driving is a good skill to have. Being able to take Zeyda to his doctor's appointments is an added family bonus."

I start the car and fasten my seat belt. "He only wants to go to the casino," I grumble.

Dad grimaces. "Fine. You can take him to the casino when you get your license."

"Just where I've always wanted to go." I start driving down our street. Slowly. So far I've only driven to and from Zeyda's house, making only right-hand turns. Dad keeps suggesting we drive over a bridge, at least, but I'm not that interested. Who needs to drive when you can bike?

Dad makes me stop in front of a grocery store, partly so he can pick up some pretzels for Zeyda, but mostly so he can force me to practice parallel parking. I'm actually good at parking—it's just geometry and spatial awareness—but I get stressed by impatient traffic waiting behind me.

When we get to Zeyda's, Dad finds a tool box in the garage and goes downstairs to look at the leaking window. Zeyda is in the small den at the front of his house, watching TV, but when he sees me, he mutes it. He seems more shrunken at this time of night. I can almost see his own fog settling into him. I imagine our two clouds joining over our heads.

"How's your mother?" Zeyda asks. "I haven't talked to her in a couple of days."

"She's good. These new Haggadahs she ordered for Passover came today, and she's excited."

Zeyda scowls, the lines between his eyes deepening. "What's wrong with the ones we always use?"

"I don't know. They're dated or something." Even though I'm supposed to be encouraging Zeyda to come to the Seder, I can't help complaining a little too. "She's also collecting costumes," I say with a shudder.

"For what?"

"Bibliodrama."

"What's that?"

I roll my eyes. "It's not enough to tell the Passover story. Mom wants the kids to act it out."

"She thinks it's a party?"

"Well, technically, a Seder *is* a party—a feast anyway. We're celebrating freedom." Zeyda's scowl deepens. "Don't worry," I tell him. "Some of her crazier ideas are already squashed. For a while she wanted everyone to sit on the floor on cushions around a low table, because that's how the Greeks used to eat."

Zeyda rolls his eyes. "Greeks? Passover is Jewish."

"Apparently the whole idea of a Seder comes from the Greek tradition. But we're not going to sit on the floor because Todd Davis has a bad back, and it wouldn't work for you either."

Zeyda looks like he might spit with disgust. "And how's Abby?"

"Busy," I say.

"Doing what?"

Busy reclaiming the word *cunt*.

Zeyda is expecting me to say more, so I change the topic. "Have you thought about going to the JCC?"

Zeyda scowls. "No. How's your boyfriend?"

"Um, not great."

Zeyda sighs. "Relationships are hard."

"Yes," I manage to murmur.

"Even Crystal and I fight like an old married couple sometimes," he says. This makes me smile. "Did he stop sending you funny pictures?" Zeyda asks.

"No. It's just...complicated."

Zeyda pats my hand. "I'll send you flowers. For you, roses."

For some reason this makes tears start to form in my eyes. I duck my head and look away from Zeyda. He squeezes my hand tightly.

I feel a blanket of sadness settle over both of us, and we sit in the gloom a long time, our fogs hovering over us. The room gets dim, but neither of us mentions putting on the lamps. Then Zeyda turns the TV volume back up, and we sit in the dark and watch the business channel until Dad says it's time to go.

Dad drives home because it's dark out, and my learner's license only covers daytime driving. Luckily, with Dad you don't always have to talk, and we're mostly silent. Being with Zeyda has made the fog thicker. I want to go home and lie in my bed and stop pretending to be cheerful or communicative, but Sofia texts, asking for math help. By the time we get home, she's waiting for me on the front steps of our house.

"I'm going to fail my quiz tomorrow if I can't figure out quadratic equations," she announces cheerfully. "Will you help me?" I say sure and we head into the house. As we make our way downstairs we hear voices from the rec room—Abby and Sunita and the other girls rehearsing their monologues.

"What's going on?" Sofia asks.

"Play rehearsal," I say.

"For what?"

"You don't want to know."

Sofia pokes me in the side. "Tell me."

I groan. "They're writing monologues about…about their vaginas for the senior drama festival."

Sofia stops on the stairs. "You're kidding."

"I wish."

"That's so awesome."

"No, it's not. It's gross." I continue down the stairs and open the door to my bedroom, but Sofia stops outside the rec room. "Wait, I want to hear." She perches herself on the bottom stair, ear cocked.

I reluctantly join her. "What about the math?" I whisper.

"After. Shh."

"My monologue is about girls and their desires," Sunita is saying, "about things we want to do, and how we don't want to be seen as objects. It's called 'I Am A Sexual Being.'"

Sofia grabs my hand and squeezes it tightly. I want to pull my sweater over my head.

Sunita reads in a loud dramatic voice, "Sometimes I think boys only see girls as objects, as things to collect. You know, the boys who have pictures of topless girls on their phones or across their bedroom walls. Sometimes I think that's all girls are to those guys, things to be traded, looked at, like baseball cards."

I sigh and resign myself to listening. I can handle a monologue about the objectification of women.

Sunita continues. "Us girls, we are not just breasts, not just a picture in your magazine or on your phone. I am not only a body, but also a mind and a face. I breathe and love and talk and am in the world, same as you. I am not just a projection for your fantasies, not just skin for your taking. I feel the things you feel. The anger and excitement, the thrill of the game, the anticipation of the roller coaster, the release after a long run. I feel all those things.

"And like you, I crave skin and body. I don't only exist to be the object of your desire. I am a sexual being in my own right. I want to be a lover, not only the loved. I wear sexy clothes for me, not for you. I am a living, breathing creature. I am a sexual being. I am in charge of my own body and all it wants. I live and I breathe and I feel, and I crave too."

There's a pause and Abby says something I can't hear, and then everyone laughs. Sofia punches a fist in the air.

"That was amazing!" she whisper-hisses. "I can't believe your sister and her friends talk about that kind of stuff. We *need* to talk about this stuff."

I pull Sofia into my room and close the door. "No, we don't."

"Please! Guys talk about these things all the time." She gives me a knowing look.

I know what she means. Last year Sofia and I were lying on the lawn outside her building when we accidentally overheard these guys talking while they waited for the bus on the other side of the hedge. At first we were annoyed by how loud they were, but then they started talking about which girls gave blow jobs, and we couldn't stop listening. They talked about some video they'd seen and what the girl was wearing and what porny things she did. Then we heard them looking at pictures of girls on their phones and saying what they'd like to do to them. Finally the bus came, and they went away. I felt like I'd been punched in the gut after listening to that conversation.

"Girls should talk about their bodies," Sofia announces, plunking herself down on my bed. "I can't wait to see your sister's play."

I sit down next to her. "The school banned it from the festival, so now they're planning some guerrilla pop-up performance. I don't know when that will be."

Sofia's eyes sparkle. "That's even cooler."

I tug on my hair. "Ugh. It's not."

Sofia lies back on my bed and tucks her hands behind her head. "You have the coolest sister."

I mock punch Sofia in the arm. "Do you want help with the math now?"

Sofia groans. "It's so boring. I totally don't get how you can be good at this stuff." She shoves her binder off the bed and onto the floor. "If you wrote a monologue, what would it be about?"

"I would never write a monologue," I say flatly.

"Oh, come on, what if you wrote a secret one?"

I lie down next to her and prop my chin in my hand. A secret monologue? I think about what I wrote in my journal about our sex-ed classes. I could call it "The Most Dangerous Thing." I imagine Paul's fingers working through my hair, and a feeling of bliss comes over me, then confusion. "I guess I'd write about relationships," I say. "How hard they are."

"Oh." Sofia's face softens. "Did you see Paul again today?"

I nod.

"How did it go?"

"Um, not so good." I swipe at tears that are starting to form.

"What happened?" Sofia sits up next to me.

I struggle to find the right words. "It's the same thing as the other day. I'm not good with people."

"You have to stop saying that. You're awesome with some people, the *right* people."

I rub my eyes again so I don't have to look at her. "This boyfriend thing. I don't really get how it works."

Sofia smiles. "Well, you hang out and do stuff together, like friends."

"Okay, I'm fine with that part."

"And then you get to do the in-love, or in-lust, stuff too. If you want to."

"That's the part I'm not good at," I whisper.

I'm expecting Sofia to prod me on this, to want details, but instead she stands up. "See, that's exactly what my monologue would be about. Girls don't talk about this stuff, about what they want, and then when they're with some guy, they don't know how to get what they want or what they need. For example, did I ever tell Carlos what I wanted him to do to me? Of course not—that would have been awkward." Sofia flips her hair out of her face. "But if you do stuff that, you know, feels good to you, then you're a whore, and his friends get to say porny things about you. And if you say no, because maybe you don't want to do those things, then you're cold or a tease. You can't win." Sofia throws her arms up in the air.

I mull this over. I don't think I could ever tell a guy what I wanted—at least, not out loud.

Sofia continues, "Boys get blow jobs, and what do girls get? Nothing, usually. Lately I've been thinking this is a social-justice issue."

"Please." I groan. "You should go and hang out with Abby."

I pick up Sofia's math binder from the floor. "Equations," I say. "We should get you ready for tomorrow."

Sofia sighs. "Fine. But later, when I've understood this stuff, I'm going home to write my own monologue. It's going to be about girls' bodies and what they can do."

I resist sticking my fingers in my ears.

Later, after Sofia has gone home and I'm finally alone in bed, I think about Sunita's monologue. I've never seen myself as an object, as something that guys might look at. I'm not the kind of person who attracts attention, who other people look at and admire. But the second part, the feeling part, that's me now, even if I don't want it to be. That feeling part wants to be with Paul all the time, to touch his skin and inhale his scent, and it's knocking me off my feet, like I'm falling off my bike every time I go downhill. When I think of Paul, I'm out of breath and want to slink close to him, yet I don't know how. I can't talk to anyone about this, not even Sofia. I am a living, breathing creature, but I also don't know how to be that creature. A layer of fog comes over me, enveloping me like a second skin, pushing me hard against my bed. I want to peel it off, but it presses dark and heavy, like it'll never go away.

Nine

I WAKE UP THE NEXT MORNING when it's still dark out, and before I even open my eyes I can feel the weight of the fog pressing down on me. The fog has grown overnight, and not only is it drifting around me like a shadow; it's filling the whole room. It takes all my concentration to keep pushing it up so it doesn't become part of me. I try to reach my phone, but my limbs are too heavy. Even opening my eyelids feels too hard. Fine. I'll will myself out of bed without Sudoku, with only my mind. I try to envision my plan: do well at school, graduate, get into business school, get a great job, buy the dream condo—but now the condo feels like a prison I'll return to every night, and I'll still be lonely because I won't be able to talk to people, and I still won't be able to get out of bed.

I watch the minutes advance on my alarm clock until it's seven. Then I hear Abby in the bathroom, and voices and footsteps overhead. If I don't get out of bed soon, I'm going to be late. I manage to roll over and pick up my phone. I text Sofia: **Give me one reason why I should get out of bed this morning.**

She writes back, **Because you have assignments due? Not good enough.**

Because I want to see what you're wearing?

Sweats.

That is sad. How about because I love you and I'll be lonely without you.

I want to write **Not good enough**, but I don't want to hurt Sofia's feelings, so I write **Thanks.** Then I tuck the phone under my pillow. Fine. The fog wins. I stop trying to push it away and let it sink into me. It feels good to stop fighting. I won't ever be able to have a boyfriend or let anyone touch me. I'll just have to accept that. I am a heavy person, and my mind is a dark cloud. It's kind of a meditation, letting the darkness ooze through me so that even my fingers and toes are filled with the cloud. It's not even sadness anymore—it's just dark. I pull the sheet over my head and hope I fall asleep and never wake up again.

Abby knocks on my door about twenty minutes later and sticks her head in my room. She's already showered and ready for breakfast. "Hey, did you sleep in?"

"No, I'm sick," I mumble from under the covers.

"Oh, do you want tea or something?"

"No."

"You don't sound sick."

"Please leave me alone."

Abby goes upstairs. I'm sure she's talking to Mom, who must be already finishing her coffee and getting ready to go. *Please leave me alone.* No such luck. Mom comes downstairs and sits on the end of my bed.

"Tell me what's wrong," she says.

"I feel sick," I mumble, the sheet still over my head.

"Like vomiting sick or flu-ish? Have you got a cold?" Mom peels the covers back and lays her hand on my forehead like the professional nurse she is. "You're not hot, and you don't look congested or nauseous," she says.

"I have bad cramps," I lie.

"Are you sure that's it?"

I nod. Mom looks at me for a moment. "Are you sure something else isn't bothering you? Do you need to go back to Dr. Spenser?"

"My mental health is perfectly fine," I whisper.

"'Cause if it's not—"

"It's fine."

"Well, take something for the cramps and get yourself to school. I'll text you in an hour."

"Okay."

The house gets quiet, and I drift in and out of sleep. I turn my phone off and shove it under my bed. The landline rings, and I ignore that too. At lunch Abby comes home and knocks on my door. She holds out her phone to me. "Mom's worried about you, so she asked me to come home and check on you. She's on the phone."

"Oh." I take the phone and sink back into bed. "Hi."

"Syd, I wish you would answer your phone."

"I was sleeping," I say.

"Are you going to get up and get yourself to school for the afternoon?"

"I don't think so."

There's a pause, and Mom asks, "What's going on?"

I don't answer right away. "I need some time alone."

"For how long, Syd?"

I hesitate. I want to say for a week, but then Mom will be really worried. "I'm sure I'll feel better tomorrow," I lie.

Mom sighs. "I'm calling Dr. Spenser."

"Please don't do that. I'll call her if I need to."

"No, I think you need help."

"I don't want help."

Mom sighs. "Okay, I'll email her and ask her to call you to check in. Okay?"

"It's not okay. Please go away," I whisper.

"Turn your phone on so your sister can go back to school. I'll text you in an hour."

I hand Abby the phone without looking at her.

"Do you want soup or something?" she asks quietly.

I shake my head and crawl back under the covers. It's dark in bed and more comfortable than the closet.

I hear Abby leave my room, go up the stairs and then out the front door.

The house is quiet until my phone rings. I don't pick up. Finally I retrieve my phone from under the bed and read Mom's texts. **Dr. Spenser says you're not picking up the phone. She's going to text you. Please respond.**

I groan and roll over. Dr. Spenser writes. **Hi, Sydney, your mom is worried about you so I said I'd check in with you. How are you feeling today?**

Like a flat board. Like a piece of run-over cardboard. Like something that doesn't exist anymore except for a snarling mind with a marble spiraling around and around: I'll never be a lover, never be loved. **Fine, thank you.** Pass go and collect two hundred dollars.

Why don't you come in tomorrow afternoon and we'll talk, Dr. Spenser writes back.

Thank you for your concern, but it's all butterflies and unicorns with me these days.

Mom texts me a few minutes later. **I made an appointment with Dr. Spenser for you tomorrow at 4 pm. Be home to hug you soon.**

My phone goes quiet, and time slides away from me like eggs off a plate. I try to read my poetry anthology, but I doze off. I'm aware of people coming home, of my door opening and then closing. At some point I fall into a deeper sleep, because when I wake up it's dark and my clock says 11:30 PM. I take inventory of how I feel. Maybe I was only tired and I've slept off the fog, and I'll wake as a new person. No such luck. My head feels like I've got bricks instead of brains. Even my mouth feels like someone stuffed paper in it while I was sleeping. I'm too heavy to move, so I lie listening to my stomach rumble for half an hour before I force myself to roll out of bed and crawl up the stairs.

The house is quiet and dark, the kitchen only illuminated by the clock on the microwave and the fridge light when I open the door. I feel dizzy from not eating, so after my eyes adjust to the darkness I sit on the floor, nibbling cheese and crackers. I listen to the night sounds—the clock ticking, the fridge humming, a dog outside in the lane. I'm not sleepy, so I watch an hour of TV, mindless home-renovation shows and infomercials for dance weight-loss programs and pressure cookers. I try to write about the darkness of the night, about the fog, how it creeps and builds and thickens. *My head like a brick, like a thickness I can't shake, like a mist wrapping about my feet and rising up, like a cloud I can't step out of.* Everything I write is exceptionally bad. The wrinkled stubs of the pages I ripped out from the "I Fear" free-write are like a scar in my book. The journal falls open to those pages from the stress on the binding, reminding me of everything I can't deal with. What I wrote about not being able to get up has come true.

I finally sleep again in the early morning, more out of desire not to face the next day than out of exhaustion. When I awake midmorning, the fog is so thick I am the fog.

I feel strangely weightless and yet very dense. I don't think I can move. The house is quiet, daylight pricking around my blinds. A stream of texts litters my phone.

Are you there Syd? Sofia texts.

Picking you up at 3:30 xoxo, Mom writes.

Hey, Sydney, I hope you're feeling better, Paul texts.

Zeyda leaves a message on my voice mail. "Nu, what happened to you yesterday? Not even a phone call to say you weren't coming? I want to know how your portfolio is performing." I had completely forgotten about the contest.

Abby has emailed me a link to a dance video. *Movement makes people feel better,* she writes.

Hours pass. I'm amazed at how little I can do. I can't move because I am nothing but fog. Around noon I get hungry enough to get out of bed and crawl upstairs for cereal. I have three and a half hours until Mom arrives to take me to Dr. Spenser. And if I refuse to talk, what happens then? Talking doesn't help—it only makes me feel ashamed. Only movement helps, the kind that is so all-consuming it dulls other sensations.

Yes, movement. I would like to move, to get off the floor, to feel like the dancers in Abby's videos, fluid and powerful, instead of the wooden block that I am. I haven't responded to any of the texts. I call Fen instead, even though he's in class.

Fen doesn't pick up, so I keep trying until he does.

"Why are you calling me now?" he says when he finally answers, sounding exasperated. "You know I'm in

French—I had to ask to go to the *toilette*, but Madame Govier totally knows what I'm up to."

"I'm sorry, but I need help."

"Why aren't you at school? Are you sick?"

"Sort of."

"What's up?" Fen asks.

"I need to go biking."

"Great, Syd. I'll meet you at three thirty."

"No, I need to go now."

"Now? What about school?"

"Fuck it. I need movement."

Fen sighs. "I know how you feel. I forgot to take my meds the other day, and I was a disaster."

"Will you come with me?"

There's a pause, and Fen says, "Where are we going?"

"I don't know. Somewhere out of the city."

Fen waits for me to say something else, to suggest a route. When he realizes I don't have any ideas, he says, "Okay, give me a couple of minutes and I'll call you back."

I lie on the kitchen floor and stare at the ceiling. I don't want to talk to Dr. Spenser. Even if I don't have to make eye contact with her, I hate talking about this thing. What if I refuse to get out of bed? Would an ambulance take me away and put me in the psych ward? My breathing starts to speed up, and I recognize the signs of a downhill slide. *Oh good god, please call back, Fen.*

I count to one hundred, but Fen doesn't call.

I take out my journal. *Fenny, henny, savior, penny.* Still the phone doesn't ring. Okay, worst-case scenario. I'll write Dr. Spenser a letter, and if I have to go see her, I'll give it to her.

Dear Dr. Spenser,

There's a fog all around me, and it's heavy and dark and it's trying to squash me. And no matter how hard I try to be the light, to find it inside me and let it shine (like the song!), the fog is too thick. And it's hard to move when there's fog, and worse, it's hard to talk to people. They have their own lights, and they're shining on me too brightly, and they can see me (and the spinach stuck in my teeth, or the sweat under my arms), but I can't see them. And sometimes I can't even hear them. And Paul will see how broken I am. That's why being in my closet is good. There's no one there, and I don't have to be anything. So can I just stay in the closet? I could set up a whole world in there. Abby could bring me food, like falafel and tabbouleh, and palak paneer with naan, and some days yogurt parfait with strawberries and granola, and if I wasn't freaked out, I might even be interested in eating. I could do online investing and maybe market analysis, all from my own little hovel. And since work would be on my own schedule, I could bike a lot. Maybe I could live on some island and bike there.

If only Fen would call.

I pick up my phone and text him. **Route?**

Almost got it.

My phone rings. "Okay," Fen says, "we bus to Ladner to avoid biking the tunnel, and then we go west and cross over to Westham Island. My mom took me berry picking there once."

I exhale. "What's it like?"

"Not much traffic, country roads, farms. It should take us all afternoon. Bring power bars, lots of them."

"Fen?"

"Yes?" He sounds impatient.

"Thank you."

Fen sighs. "You owe me."

"Okay."

We hang up. And then, even though it hurts to move, and even though Paul is texting me—**Where are you? Is everything okay?**—I get up and put on my bike clothes. I text Mom that I'm going biking, so she doesn't think I've disappeared or done anything weird, and then leave my phone on my bed.

Fen and I take the bus south, our bikes on the rack on the front of the bus, and then we bike through Ladner, stopping for traffic lights. Once we are on the island, my mind fills with the low, dull hum of my aching muscles, and I'm happy to feel my body complaining rather than the circular thoughts of my stupid brain. Legs, I think as I pedal, legs, legs, legs.

We pass fields with horses and cows, and I pick up a whiff of scent from an apple tree in full bloom as we bike by. Fen picks up the pace, and we race along a road by the sea. The fog doesn't lift, but under the fog I can feel my body, legs pumping, heart chugging along.

If I breathe hard enough, I might be able to blow the darkness away.

After an hour Fen slows down, and we get off our bikes by a dike and rest in the shade of a bridge. I walk around stretching out my quads while Fen inhales power bars.

"Why are we doing this on a school day?" Fen asks. "I'm missing rugby too."

"'Cause I needed to, and I couldn't do it myself."

"Oh. Okay." Fen nods. "I'm trying to find a university with the most access to biking. I figure if I could go to class for an hour and then get on my bike for an hour, I'd be good."

"Maybe you could study on a stationary bike somewhere on campus. You could sweat all day."

Fen shakes his head. "Not good enough. I'm thinking of a school somewhere in the middle of nowhere, but with good biking weather, like Colorado."

I nod. "Thanks for coming with me today."

Fen gives me a big sweaty hug, which is a little disgusting but also feels good. And it's just a hug. And I don't have to look at him while we do it.

We bike at a more leisurely pace back to Ladner, both of us having ridden out some of the things crawling up our spines. Fen is more relaxed, pedaling beside me and telling me stories about the rugby players and something he calls What Guys Do to Prove Their Manliness. When we get back on the bus, he checks his phone.

"Sofia says Paul is wondering if I know where you are. Apparently you aren't responding to texts."

"I didn't bring my phone," I say.

Fen swats me with a cycling glove. "Syd, that's too weird."

"I don't even know what time it is. Just tell them we went biking."

Fen shakes his head. "It's four thirty. Trouble in lovebird paradise?"

Four thirty. I've missed my appointment with Dr. Spenser. I turn back to Fen. "You could say that."

He types for a minute, his fingers jutting over the screen like his neck does when he's wound up. "What's up with Paul?"

"It's, well, a lot of eye contact."

"Ah, like you actually have to talk to him?"

"Yes."

Fen grins. "I can see how you would totally suck at that."

"Thanks."

"This is going to sound awful, but maybe you weren't meant to have a boyfriend. I mean, not right now."

I sigh. "I know."

"Then call it quits." Fen rubs his gloved hands together as if washing away the word *boyfriend*.

"But I like him."

"Oh. So you're caught in the middle of wanting and not wanting?"

"Pretty much."

"What are you going to do?"

"I don't know. Play hooky and go biking with you?" I step on Fen's toe lightly.

"Every day?"

I wilt a little. "I'm only dealing with today."

Fen steps on my toe, a little harder than I did his. This is the kind of boyfriend I need. Not Fenny, exactly, but one who understands communication through toe pressure.

I don't want to go home, but I'm sweaty and hungry and there's nowhere else for me to go, so Fen and I say goodbye and I bike back home. When I let myself in by the back door, Mom is sitting at the kitchen counter, in her work blouse and skirt, with Paul. I stop in the doorway and finger my sweaty ponytail. Paul looks relaxed sitting with Mom, and I wonder how long he's been here and what they've been talking about. I stand for a moment in the doorway, my heart hammering away in my chest like I'm still on my bike. "I went biking," I say stupidly.

"I see that." Mom stands and licks her lips like she does when she's pissed off. She glares at me. "I'm glad you were feeling up to it," she says, a hint of sarcasm in her voice.

"Uh, yeah," I say.

Mom starts looking less pissed off and more relieved. "Paul was telling me about the investor's club. He says you and Sofia are leading the competition."

"Zeyda's helping us," I say quietly.

"I bet," Mom says. "Sydney, can I talk to you a moment?"

I follow Mom into the front hall. I can tell from the way she walks that she's still angry with me. She stands in the front hall, hands on her hips, and whispers, "I'm going back to work for a couple of hours, since I spent most of the afternoon worrying about where you were and if you were okay."

"I'm sorry," I whisper.

Mom closes her eyes for a moment. "When you stopped responding to texts and then we couldn't find you…" She swallows back tears.

I bite my lip. "I didn't mean to make you worry."

Mom waves a hand in the air. "I'm glad you're okay." She starts putting on her coat and picking up her purse. "Now, you need to text Dr. Spenser and let her know why you missed your appointment. Then I need you to make dinner."

"Dinner?" I repeat.

"Yes, if you're up for biking, you're up for dinner. There's chicken defrosting in the fridge, and potatoes and broccoli too. Zeyda's coming."

"Zeyda's coming? He never leaves his house."

Mom cocks her head. "He said for you, he'd come. He also asked that we not make chickpeas—they give him too much gas."

"Oh," I say. "Gross. Wait, why's he coming for dinner?"

Mom steps into her heels. "It's Shabbat, and he wants to make sure you're okay. You didn't visit today or yesterday or even call. He was worried." She sighs. "We're all worried."

"Oh." I wrap my arms around myself. I was so busy thinking about myself, I didn't even remember Zeyda. I start to shiver from my cooling sweat.

"You don't feel well?" Mom says.

"Just hungry and cold. Normal stuff."

Mom chucks me under the chin, like I'm seven, and picks up her purse. "Have dinner ready for around seven, please. I'm picking up Zeyda, and we have to wait for Dad to get home from the hospice."

"Okay," I say.

Mom goes out the front door, and I wander back to the kitchen. Paul looks so cute sitting at the counter, spinning a little on the stool, holding one of Mom's ceramic mugs. I hold on to the counter to stop my hands' shaking. I'm not sure if they're shaking because I'm starving or if it's because Paul is here in my kitchen. "Did my mom make you tea?" I ask.

"She did," Paul says. "She also offered to make me a sandwich."

I move around the island to pour myself a bowl of cereal. "How long have you been here?"

"About half an hour. I hope you don't mind me showing up. I was worried you were mad at me and that's why you weren't returning my texts. I thought I might walk over."

"Not mad, just other stuff going on."

"Sofia said."

"What did Sofia say?"

"She said you were taking a few days off."

I nod. Even though Paul is watching me, I shovel cereal into my mouth, chewing quickly. I sigh as the sugars start taking effect. "I'm pretty cold." I run my hands through my sweaty hair.

"Do you want me to leave?"

"Can you wait a bit while I shower?"

Paul nods, and I leave him sitting at the counter while I go downstairs. I drum my fingers on the shower wall as the hot water pounds down on me. Paul is in my house, in my kitchen, waiting for me, and the fog might knock me down at any moment. I wash quickly, trying to use up my nervous energy. Then I pull on jeans, a sweatshirt and thick socks, and comb out my hair. I text Dr. Spenser, **Please excuse my absence today. I had a therapeutic bike session to attend.**

She writes back, **How about we talk Monday at 4 pm?**

It's really not necessary.

Come in on Monday and we'll go from there.

I shove my phone in my pocket and head back upstairs. Paul is still sitting at the counter, still making my heart pound.

"Better?" he asks.

"Yes." I put the kettle on.

"You were biking today?"

I nod. "It was necessary."

"Why biking?"

"If I move, then I don't have to think about things."

"I see." Paul looks down at his mug. "I wish you had answered my texts."

"I couldn't. I mean, I didn't know what to say."

"If you don't want me to call you or anything, I'll stop." He means if I don't like him.

"No," I say, "I want to keep hanging out."

"Oh." He looks relieved.

Fen said I wasn't ready for a boyfriend. "I think it would be okay if we did homework together and cloud-watched and played pool."

"Like, if we were friends?"

"Yeah, something like that."

Paul looks crushed.

"But not just friends." Shit, I don't have the right words for anything. "Here." I thrust a potato at him. "Can you peel this for me?"

Paul takes the potato and the peeler. I grab another peeler, and we silently make a hill of peel between us. The kitchen is full of the fog as well as the nervous energy of being with Paul. I peel furiously. "What are we making?" Paul finally asks.

"Potato kugel." I keep my head down.

"Potato what?"

"Grated potato with egg and onions. Kind of like a giant hash brown, but you bake it."

"Sounds good. What else are you cooking?"

"Chicken. Dinner can't be too adventurous because my zeyda is coming, so I'll probably roll the chicken in breadcrumbs. I'm also making broccoli and a challah."

"What's that?"

"It's this traditional bread Jewish people eat on the Sabbath. It's kind of sweet, and you braid the dough."

"Can I help you make it?"

"Sure." Mom didn't ask me to make a challah, but it seems like a good activity, something to keep me busy.

I pull out the yeast and sugar and other ingredients and talk Paul through the recipe. By the time he's finished kneading the dough, I'm exhausted—from biking, from talking, from being me. "I think I need to lie down now," I tell Paul, and he nods.

I walk him to the front door. He says, "Will I see you at school Monday?"

"Yes," I say. "My mother will kill me otherwise."

"We could work on our homework again after school."

"Maybe. There's this coffee shop on Main Street we could go to," I suggest.

Paul smiles slowly. "Like a date."

"Okay. Whatever." I step on his foot lightly.

Paul looks down. "Is that your way of saying goodbye?"

"Yes, it's Sydney-speak for goodbye."

Paul punches me gently on the shoulder. "This is Paul-speak for see you later."

I want to grab him and hug him tight. Instead I watch him amble down our front steps. Then I leave the challah to rise and collapse onto the couch in the living room and fall into a deep, dreamless sleep.

I wake with a blanket on top of me and Zeyda sitting by my feet, sipping a Scotch. Mom and Abby are in the kitchen, taking food out of the oven. Dad's setting the table.

"I didn't finish making dinner," I say.

Zeyda pats my feet. "Not to worry."

I close my eyes.

"Mom says she came home and found a boy sitting on our front steps," Abby calls from the kitchen.

"Paul?" Zeyda says.

"You know about him?" Mom and Abby say at the same time.

"Yes," Zeyda says. "A nice boy, a little strange. He likes mushrooms."

"Like, magic mushrooms?" Abby asks.

I groan and close my eyes again.

"No," Zeyda says, "the kind that grow in your lawn."

"That is strange," Abby says.

"He seems like a nice kid," Mom says. I can tell from the way she says it that she knows something is up between us.

"Paul's my lab partner," I say. "And I was with Fenny all afternoon."

"Ooh, Fen's a hottie," Abby says.

I throw a cushion in her direction.

We sit down for dinner, say the Friday-night blessings and pass the dishes around the table. There's salad as well as the chicken, potato kugel, broccoli and the challah. No one mentions that I haven't been to school in two days or that I wouldn't answer my phone all day. No one brings up Passover, and Zeyda doesn't say anything about Paul not being Jewish. After dinner we drink tea and nibble oatmeal cookies and play Bananagrams. Then Dad drives Zeyda home, and Abby disappears to practice her monologue, and it's just Mom and me at the kitchen table.

Mom looks at me. "Did you make an appointment with Dr. Spenser?"

"Yep, 4:00 PM Monday."

"Do you want me to take you?"

"Nope." I fiddle with the game tiles.

"I might drive you anyway."

"Oh." She means to make sure I go this time. "I wrote Dr. Spenser a letter, so I'm ready to see her."

"Do you want to share it with me?"

"Nope." I keep my head down.

Mom sighs. "Okay. It was nice of Paul to come and check on you."

"Yep." I add and remove tiles to make words. *Mother, other, not her, not here, her ear, not her ear.*

Mom says, "You know, you could talk to me about him or anything else, if you wanted to."

"Thanks." I move the tiles back to *not her, her ear.* I stand up. "I think I'll go to bed."

Mom nods. "Have a good sleep."

I lie awake in bed a long time, letting the darkness press down on me. Even though I didn't say much to Mom, the fact that she knows about Paul and knows I need to see Dr. Spenser makes the fog feel a little lighter.

Ten

FOR THE NEXT TWO WEEKS I see Dr. Spenser twice a week.
I tell her about the fog, and that there's a boy I like, but
that I can't get through the fog to him. This isn't exactly
true, but it's close enough, and it's better than telling her
that eye contact (and other contact) freaks me out. She
probably knows that anyway, since I spend the whole time
I'm talking to her looking at this toy she has—a fabric
bag of rice with a plastic window in it. You can move the
rice around and find little toys inside. When I discover
there's an object for each letter of the alphabet, I challenge
myself to find them in alphabetical order, which is almost
impossible. It makes talking to Dr. Spenser easier though.

And still the fog weighs me down, worse in the
morning. I force myself to eat, go to school, do my
homework, visit Dr. Spenser, take the antidepressants she
prescribes. She says they should help my anxiety as well.

I hang on to this shred of information, hoping to wake up one day and miraculously feel better, the fog cleared away like when the sun comes out after weeks of Vancouver rain. It hasn't happened yet, but I do feel the side effects, which seems unfair. The meds make me feel flat, almost dead, as if the fog is happening to someone else.

Instead of relying on Sudoku or other games to get me up in the morning, Dr. Spenser suggests I have friends check in on me. And so each morning when I get up and reach for my phone, I find a text from Sofia or Fen or sometimes Paul. Sofia writes things like **Get out of bed so you can see my fabulous new streaks.** Fen sends biking routes for a trip he's planning for us in the summer, which is something to look forward to. Paul sends his latest photos of logs on the beach. Abby's been checking in on me a lot too, making me breakfast in the morning, and Mom asks or texts me about how I feel at least ten times a day. Sometimes all the attention is a little overwhelming, but mostly it makes me feel better. When I feel like sitting in my closet and not coming out again, I try to focus on the investor's club— Sofia and I have fallen behind in the ratings—or write some new poems. I try writing about investing, but those poems are worse than anything I've come up with so far.

At home, Mom focuses on Passover and starts stockpiling special Passover foods—boxes of matzah, matzah meal, macaroons, prunes and other kosher for Passover treats. She attaches a Seder seating plan to the refrigerator and a menu—chicken soup with matzah balls,

THE MOST DANGEROUS THING

gefilte fish, charoset, brisket, arugula salad with roasted red onions, sweet-potato *tsimmes* with pears and pecans, leek and potato kugel, fruit compote and Passover brownies. My mouth waters every time I look at the list, even though I still don't have much appetite.

Zeyda and I reach a compromise about the casino. I promise Zeyda to take him if he'll try out the JCC. Zeyda agrees as long as I'm willing to drive. One Saturday afternoon I drive Zeyda's old car with Zeyda, Crystal and her son, Leonard, who has a valid driving license and likes gambling, to the casino in Richmond. I'm so nervous about driving over a bridge, making left-hand turns and going somewhere I don't know that by the time we arrive, I'm a sweaty mess. Leonard helps Zeyda lose his money in the casino, and Crystal and I spend the afternoon at a nearby mall. A few days later Zeyda goes to the JCC senior hour with Crystal. When I arrive at Zeyda's house that same day, Zeyda is thrilled to announce he won seventy-five dollars playing cards against Abe Sandler. This is less than he lost at the casino, but Zeyda doesn't care. Abe Sandler calls while I'm visiting to insist on a rematch the following week. After a long conversation of insults and reminiscing, Zeyda turns to me and says with gusto, "I'm going to bleed that sucker dry."

Paul's mom arrives in Vancouver, so I mainly see him at school. We work on a chem lab at Starbucks after school one day, and one Saturday we go down to Granville Island to eat lunch and watch the seagulls and the buskers. He kisses me goodbye, but it's on Main Street, and we don't linger. Instead of hanging out with him, I spend time with Dr. Spenser.

Dr. Spenser wants to talk about how I feel, and I only want to know when the meds are going to kick in.

"So I should definitely feel better by the end of the month, right?" I'm in Dr. Spenser's office after school, slumped in a black-leather swivel chair.

"Yes," she says. "It might take a while to get the dosage right."

"Like, how long?" I persist.

"There's no hard-and-fast rule."

I sink further in my chair. "Can I hide in my closet until that happens?"

"You could, but that doesn't sound like very much fun."

"Have you tried going out in the world when you feel like this?" I can't help the angry edge in my voice.

Dr. Spenser leans back in her chair and looks me straight in the eye. "I understand how hard this must be, Syd, but you have to understand that meds aren't going to fix everything. You also need to get out and be involved in your life."

"Involved in my life?"

"Yes. The more you engage with the world, the better you're going to feel."

I don't answer. The fog is so thick I can't see past it.

Dr. Spenser continues. "Sitting in your closet is only going to make you feel worse."

"It's just a last resort," I mumble. "I only do it once or twice a week."

Dr. Spenser nods. "Good. What else do you do that makes you feel better?"

I swivel my chair back and forth before answering. "I hang out with my zeyda. We do investing together."

"What about kids your own age?"

"Well, I bike with Fen, and Sofia and I hang out."

"And there's Paul too, right?"

I look down at my lap. "Yeah, him too."

"That's not going well?"

"It's complicated."

There's a long silence. Dr. Spenser waits patiently. She doesn't even tap a pen on the desk or look at me. Finally I say, "It's hard to be with him."

"What's stopping you?" she asks quietly.

"I can't say."

"Think about it," she says. "Maybe you'll tell me next time. Or maybe you could write about it."

I stand up to go, but before I get to the door, Dr. Spenser says, "Sometimes you just need to let people into your life. Take a risk."

I nod and swallow back tears. If I let Paul be close to me and it doesn't go well, I might never get out of my closet.

The next day in writing class, Mrs. Lee starts with another free-write exercise. I haven't done much writing in the last couple of weeks, and I'm behind on my poetry assignment. Mrs. Lee says this will be our final free-write this term. I sigh and pick up my pen. I hope it will be something impersonal, like a list of red things, or a writing prompt like "I See." But Mrs. Lee says we should start with "I Want." I take my time opening my journal and choosing a pen, and then I tap the pen on the page. Everyone else has already started. I pretend to think. Finally, I start writing.

I want to live alone and go biking every day. I want tomato soup and Saltines for lunch, and to never have to go to therapy again. I want to go on a long biking trip with Fen or to the beach in Croatia with Sofia. I want Passover to be over and Abby's play to disappear with the fog. I want to not exist some of the time. I want a walk-in closet. I shake my hand out. *I want to study commerce and take Zeyda on a cruise. I want to walk on the beach and for the rain to stop and the weather to be warm.* I take a break for a minute. All this stuff is true, but none of it is very interesting. I take a deep breath and keep going. *I want to be with Paul and for it not to be hard. I want to be the kind of person who laughs and tells jokes and even skips. Yes, I want to skip, with Paul.* I pause and imagine this. *And after we're done skipping, I want to disappear with him into his basement, back to that couch, back to his skin.* I feel my cheeks heat up, and I put down my pen. I think about sex-ed class, about girls' desires. That could go right in this free-write. Instead I write, *I want this exercise to finish, for Mrs. Lee to say stop.* All around me people are still scribbling and tapping. I turn to a fresh page in my book. *I want a pumpkin-caramel muffin, Earl Grey tea, French toast, seared green beans and a rare steak.* I fill the rest of the page with food items until Mrs. Lee says stop.

When the bell rings I shove the journal in my bag and get out of class as quickly as I can.

The next day at lunch there's a commotion in the hallway, students all heading in one direction. "What's that about?" Sofia asks Fen and me.

"I'm not sure," I say, but I have a bad feeling.

"Maybe this?" Fen holds up his phone and shows us a Facebook invitation: *The Vagina Stories, NOT a Drama Festival production.* It's happening today, right now, in the drama studio.

"Oh, this is so exciting," Sofia cries out.

"Ugh, I can't believe she's actually doing this," I wail. "Let's leave the building."

"Yeah right," Sofia says. She grabs my hand and drags me down the hall along with the herd of kids.

I follow reluctantly. A crowd gathers outside the drama studio as students slowly file in past a sign on the wall announcing the performance. Sofia, Fen and I go in and stand at the back, behind kids sitting on the amphitheater-style stairs that lead down to the stage where

Abby and her cast sit on wooden chairs, dressed in black. Outside the room someone yells, "Vaginas," and other kids hoot. Then an usher closes the door and the lights dim except for a spotlight on Sunita, who begins the opening monologue. She stands with her hands on her hips, one foot cocked to the side, and begins.

"Sometimes I think boys only see girls as objects, as things to collect." Even though Sunita looks confident, almost cocky, I grab Sofia's hand, squeeze it tightly and stare down at my shoes, too embarrassed to look.

I try not to hear Sunita's words, but I can't help it. The students listen, the studio silent, and then Mr. Edwards pokes his head into the room. I watch him take in Abby and her friends. I wonder if he gave Abby permission. From the surprised look on his face, I think not. He surveys the room, the quiet audience. Maybe he'll pretend he didn't see. Maybe he'll get in his car and drive to McDonald's for lunch. *I wasn't on school property,* he'll say. *I didn't know it was going on.*

Sunita finishes her monologue. Then Abby gets up, the spotlight shining on her golden hair. I feel my guts tighten. I want to slip out and not hear her words. When she speaks her first line, "My grandmother could never say the word *vagina,*" I want to sink through the floor. I push myself behind Sofia and Fen. "I can't believe she's doing this," I mutter. Sofia shushes me. When Abby says the word *cunt,* a murmur goes through the room. Abby waits for it to subside before going on.

And then there are footsteps coming down the hallway, not the shuffling and ambling of student sneakers making their way to lunch or stopping to talk to friends, but hard-soled shoes marching down the hall with intent. I hear them stop, and then I hear the sound of a poster being ripped off the wall. I cringe and dig my fingers into Sofia's palm. She squeals a little. Then the lights flip on, and the principal, Mr. Gupta, uses his super-loud voice to interrupt Abby. "Show's over, folks. Please head back to your usual lunch spots."

Abby turns to Mr. Gupta. "For some of us, this is our usual lunch spot."

"Not today it isn't."

Students start filing out of the room. I linger behind but slip out when Mr. Gupta glares at me.

When we're back on the third floor, in front of our lockers, Sofia says, "Your sister is one brave cunt. I'm going to have to design a whole line of Abby-inspired clothes."

I slump against my locker and slide to the floor. "Please, no genital-inspired T-shirts." I've tried texting Abby twice since the show got shut down, but she hasn't responded. Sofia shows me a whole thread of Facebook cunt talk already going on. Things like *drama cunts performing at school.* It's mostly silly stuff, and Abby will be pissed because none of it addresses her concerns about women.

"Did you ever write your own monologue?" Sofia asks.

"Yeah right," I say.

"I'm going to write mine today," Sofia declares.

I don't pay too much attention to her, but after school Sofia convinces me to go to the mall to look at shoes. She's been doing this a lot lately, trying to keep me busy. After a few stores we end up ordering hot-fudge brownies in White Spot. As soon as we sit down in the booth, Sofia whips a notebook out of her backpack. "I wrote my mono-logue," she says.

"Didn't you have class this afternoon?"

"I wrote it instead of taking math notes."

"That's great, Sof." I sip my water. "But I think you're a little late for the performance."

"It doesn't matter. I want you to hear it."

I groan. "Do I have to?"

She grins. "Yes."

"Here?" I look around the restaurant. Luckily there's no one sitting near us.

"Yep."

I slide down a little in the booth. "Okay, fine. I'm listening, but whisper, okay?"

Sofia nods. "Right, a quiet little vagina monologue." She smiles self-consciously. "It's called 'Finding Your Magic Button.'" She begins reading quietly. "Every girl has a button, but lots of girls don't know where to find it. Some don't even know it exists. It's kind of hidden away, but it's a super thing, if you can find it. It's kind of like a magic button. If you press it, great things can happen."

I clap a hand over my mouth. "I know you think girls should talk about these things," I hiss, "but *here*, in White Spot?"

"I'm whispering," she says, "and no one is around us. Just listen."

I grip the table. "Is it long?"

"No, just listen. If you press it, great things can happen. Girls should take the time to find their magic buttons so they can know what they like, and then maybe they can share that knowledge with someone *they* like. Then they can say, 'Push my button.'" Sofia closes her notebook. "That's it."

I sit with my mouth hanging open.

"Aren't you going to say something?" she asks.

I swallow. "Um, well, at least you didn't use the m-word?"

"You mean masturbation," she says too loudly.

"Please, stop!"

She laughs. "I won't say it again. Not even to bug you. How's your monologue?"

"The one I said I wasn't writing?"

Sofia bats a hand in the air.

I stand up in the booth. "I think I see the waiter coming."

She arches one eyebrow at me. "Chicken."

I sit down and raise an eyebrow back at her. "Chicken?"

"Yep."

"Is that a challenge?"

Sofia nods. "I challenge you to write your own mono-logue—on relationships or sex or whatever."

"I can write on whatever?"

"Sure."

"How about brownies?"

"Your own *vagina* monologue."

I wrinkle my brow. Then the waiter comes with our order. I take a large spoonful of the rich cake. "I'll think about it," I tell Sofia.

She nods. "Good enough."

The house is empty when I get home from the mall. Mom texts me to let me know she and Dad are still at a meeting at school with Abby and the principal and that they'll pick up something for dinner. I sense it's going to be a long evening. I'd like to crawl into bed, even though it's only 5:00 PM, pull the covers over my head and pretend the day didn't happen. I know the fog will creep up on me if I do that, so I wander around the house for a few minutes. I consider going to Zeyda's even though it's late in the day. I've been biking to his house a lot so I can exhaust myself and get Zeyda some fresh air—now that the weather is nicer, I've been trying to take him for regular walks along the beach.

I sit down at the kitchen table with my homework. I work through a few math problems and then glance at my writing journal. The due date for the poetry assignment is coming up. Mrs. Lee says if we're stuck we should look back through our free-writes, which I'd rather not do. And Sofia wants me to write a vagina monologue. I grimace and flip back to the page where I wrote about the dangers of sex ed.

I reread the lines, adding a few ideas and crossing out some words. *What if the most dangerous part of sex isn't pregnancies or possible infection? What if the most dangerous thing is ourselves? Our own desires? No one talks about these. We pretend girls don't have them. But what if we did? What if we talked about the dangers of sex, but also the*

I get stuck thinking of a word. Pleasure? *Sounds like please her, her pleas, sure.* I tap a line of dots across the page with my pen. Then I cross out *pleasure*. It sounds too much like something you'd read in a dorky women's magazine. *What if we talked about the dangers of sex for girls, but also the bliss?* I put down my pen and look at *bliss* written on my page. I don't hate it. Then I write, *Bliss from a kiss, your hands promise more. But a kiss is also an abyss, your hands. Is a kiss bliss?*

I put down my pen and reread these lines. I could maybe send these to Sofia, if I worked on them more. I think she'd like them. Dr. Spenser would probably like to read them too.

Abby and her friends get an in-school suspension, the most annoying punishment. You don't get to stay home, and you have to bug all your teachers for assignments so you don't get behind. Not that Abby cares about falling behind or bothers to do any work. She spends her suspension blogging about the play and trying to get *Bitch* and *Ms.* to pick up her story. She calls the local TV station, and they interview her while she's on suspension, which, as my mother says, is true chutzpah. She doesn't make the six o'clock news, which was her goal, but she does get a small article in *The Sun,* which invites people to write in their opinions. Abby is horrified when almost all the people who write in side with the administration. *That kind of play has no place at school,* writes one indignant person. Abby is so angry she designs a cunt T-shirt, but Mom and Dad finally step in before she has it printed. "People will think it's a swearword and nothing else," Mom reasons.

Abby tries to get in the news again, but she's already last week's story. Parents not allowing their teenage daughters to wear a T-shirt with the word *cunt* across the front is not news. Abby refuses to go to school. "I am so angry," she says, "at everyone!"

She fills the house with so much anger and frustration that I almost feel like moving in with Zeyda to get away from her. She takes over our whole rec room with her friends, her noise and her vagina songs. By the weekend her passion and anger fizzle out, and she's in the tent binge-watching episodes of *Glee*, pages of her monologues and protest letters scattered around her. Fen is out of town with his father, biking on one of the Gulf Islands, so there's no Saturday-morning bike ride, and Sofia is busy working on an art project. Passover begins Tuesday night, so Mom asks me to help her do some cleaning. I think she means light dusting or sweeping, and I agree to help until I realize "cleaning" means ripping apart the kitchen in a maniacal search for any kind of bread, cake, cookies, pasta, crackers or flour and packing it up in boxes to rid the house of any *chametz*—foods not kosher for Passover.

I wander around the house for a while, then try to do some writing, but I have nothing to say. I feel like crawling into my bed or hiding out in my closet for the weekend, but then I'll never get out Monday morning. I write a text to Dr. Spenser—**When did you say I'll feel better?**—but I don't send it. I need to go somewhere or do something different. I find Dad in the yard and beg him to take me biking somewhere outside the city. When he sees Mom pulling all the dishes out of the cupboards to wipe the shelves clean, he agrees. By the time Dad has the bikes loaded onto the car, the kitchen looks like a bomb has gone off in it.

Instead of driving east or south, Dad decides to drive us to West Vancouver. Traffic is slow over the Lions Gate

Bridge, and I'm doubtful about biking any of the hilly, narrow roads along the coast, but when we finally start biking the lower level of Marine Drive, going toward Horseshoe Bay, I forget my earlier impatience, and my head starts to clear. On my left the sun glints off the ocean. Islands dot the horizon, with the mountains gleaming in the background, their snowcapped tops like icing. For once I don't lose myself in my burning quads and racing breath—I can't stop looking around, can't stop breathing in all the beauty.

When we get to Horseshoe Bay, Dad and I sit on a park bench by the water and watch the ferries come in. We sip from our water bottles and eat the nut mix Dad brought.

"What a beautiful ride," I say.

Dad grins. "I thought you'd like it."

I take off my helmet and run my fingers through my sweaty hair. "Thank you for getting me away from Mom and Abby." *Thank you for getting me away from the fog.*

Dad laughs and shakes his head. "They both have a lot of passion."

I grimace. "I wish Abby could be passionate in a less embarrassing way."

Dad stretches his arms above his head. "Oh, she's just fighting for what she believes in."

"More attention for Abby?"

"That's not fair," Dad says. "Your sister is passionate about getting respect for women's bodies. That's a noble pursuit."

I give Dad my *you're kidding* look.

Dad sighs. "No, really. Remember last year when Abby found the afikoman at the Seder?"

I nod. Every year the Seder leader hides a piece of matzah, called the afikoman, for the kids to find and exchange for money. Last year, instead of giving the kids the money, Dad decided he would make a donation to a charity instead. When Abby found the matzah, she asked Dad to donate to a women's shelter.

Dad continues, "So I wrote a check to the shelter. Then about two weeks later, they called to personally thank me. They insisted on telling me exactly how my money had been spent and how my donation was helping rescue women from abusive situations. I wanted to put your sister on the phone instead, but she wasn't home."

I'm not sure why Dad is telling me this long story, but I keep listening.

"Anyway," Dad says, "they weren't calling only to thank me, but to ask for more money to help other women. They were very descriptive about the abuses women were suffering, and very persuasive. They said things like, *Mr. Mizner, there are women right now being abused and you can help them.* They told me about a woman who came to them with a broken arm. She couldn't hold her toddler. They said, *We're helping her because of you.*"

"Did you give them more money?" I ask.

Dad nods. "I send a monthly amount now. I couldn't listen without being moved. And so when your sister wants to talk about women, and their bodies"—I squirm hearing Dad say this—"I feel I should support her."

"Wow," I say.

"Yeah," Dad says. "Your sister made change happen through our family."

"I still don't know why she can't write letters to the editor or something less embarrassing."

Dad grins. "Putting on a play, even an embarrassing one, is a good way to educate a lot of people. Besides, we all have to fight the good fight our own way."

"We do?" I say.

"Sure. The play is Abby's way of doing tikkun olam. Working at the hospice is mine."

Tikkun olam means "repairing the earth" or "fixing the world." It's weird to hear Dad using Hebrew. He almost never does. Even when he sings along at shul or at Friday-night dinner, he keeps his voice low, a sort of under-the-covers singing.

"Is that what you're doing at the hospice?" I ask.

"Yes. When your mom decided to join her new shul, she asked if I would add something Jewish to my life too. Your mom likes to be Jewish through prayer and song and ritual, but that's not my thing. So I chose the hospice."

"I don't get it. What does the hospice have to do with being Jewish?"

"Visiting the sick is one of the highest commandments," Dad says.

"Oh, right." The commandments are the list of things Jews are supposed to do. It starts with the basic ten—don't kill, honor your parents, et cetera—and then there are another 603. "Do you like going to the hospice?" I ask Dad.

Dad rubs his sweaty beard and then sips his water before answering. "Well, at first I dreaded it, but now I'm more used to it. I still feel uncomfortable knowing those people are dying, but I feel like I make a small difference."

I think for a moment, watching the seagulls wheel out over the sea, squawking to each other. "You think Abby's play is a form of activism?"

"Yeah, I do. She's trying to fix the world. You know, there's a long history of Jewish activism. I think it's as important as praying or learning the Torah."

I nod. When Dad calls Abby's play activism, it makes it seem less crazy.

Dad squeezes my shoulder. "What about you?"

"What do you mean?"

"I mean, what's your passion?"

I shrug. This reminds me of Dr. Spenser telling me I need to be involved in my life. I could say riding my bike is my passion. Once I would have said making money so I could be rich enough to escape into my own fortress. Now I'm just trying to hold things together. I say, "I don't know. I have this ongoing project with Dr. Spenser."

Dad squeezes my shoulder again. "Well, that's where you are right now, but it doesn't mean you'll always be there. Sometimes getting out of yourself helps."

I look away, feeling uncomfortable. Dad and I have never talked about what I call The Day the Fog Won.

Dad stands up and clips on his bike helmet. "You're still being helpful, like the way you visit Zeyda and help Mom with her Seder."

I shudder. "Please don't remind me of the Seder."

Dad grins. "Oh, come on. I'm sure it'll be fun."

I shudder again.

We get back on our bikes and start for home, the sun lower in the sky now. I think about Dad feeding patients in the hospice and Mom planning her Seder and Abby working on her play. They each have their own thing. Dad wants to know what my thing is going to be. Maybe after I go to business school and get a great job, I'll be rich enough to donate a lot of money to whatever charity I think is best. Maybe something to do with population control or shoes for poor people. Maybe, but it doesn't feel like this is going to be enough.

By the time we get home, Mom has put the kitchen back together but has taped a Do Not Open sign on the newly cleaned cupboards where the Passover food waits to be eaten.

She's relegated the flour, crackers, rice and other carbs to a box in the laundry room.

"What if I'm hungry for crackers before Passover starts? Does this mean I have to snack in the laundry room?" I pour myself a glass of water. My legs ache, but otherwise I feel better.

Mom lifts her head up from where she's lying on the couch, visibly exhausted. "Technically, that food doesn't belong to us anymore."

"What are you talking about?"

"I sold it," she says.

"I'm sorry, you what?"

"I sold it to the Dixons. You know, next door."

"Yes, I know who the Dixons are, but I don't know why the Dixons would buy our carbs."

"Aha." Mom sits up. "They're not just carbs. They're *chametz*. It's a tradition, Sydney, to sell your chametz to someone not Jewish for the duration of Passover."

I raise my eyebrows. "How much is our box of half-used chametz worth?" I overemphasize the guttural *ch* sound.

"A dollar."

I drink my water. "Can't you get a better price?"

Mom lies back down and closes her eyes. "It's symbolic. You're still going to make the tsimmes for me, right?"

"Tsimmes. Yes. I'm on it." Tsimmes is a sweet baked dish made with carrots and prunes, but I found a new recipe with sweet potatoes, pears and pecans that sounds much better. I turn back to Mom. "What if the Dixons want to sell the food back to you for more than a dollar? What if they decide the food is actually worth ten dollars, or twenty, or if they eat all those fancy crackers from Costco? Or, worse, what if they decide to give it all away?"

"Syd," Mom says, her eyes closed.

"What?"

"Please go away."

I shrug, grab a banana and head downstairs.

Abby is still lying in front of the TV, flicking channels, her hair unwashed. She's not even wearing a colorful scarf. I understand how she feels.

"Do you want to play Scrabble?" I ask her. Abby ignores me. "How about Wii?" She closes her eyes. "Monopoly? Ping-Pong?"

She groans. "We don't have a Ping-Pong table."

"I'll let you do my hair," I say.

Abby gives me the finger.

"I was thinking about your play," I say, sitting down on the cushion next to her.

Abby shoves me away from her. "You're sweaty. Move over."

I roll off the cushion and stretch my hamstrings. "Maybe you could put on the play somewhere else, not at school."

"The play is dead," she says, eyes straight ahead.

"Did the other girls quit?" I ask.

"No."

"Then why is it dead?"

"It just is. If it's not at school, then kids won't see it."

She has a point. I get up and take a shower.

Mom doesn't want anyone eating or cooking in the newly cleaned kitchen, so we go out for Indian food at a nearby restaurant. After dinner Mom and Dad decide to go to a movie and leave Abby and me to walk home. On the way back we pass the newly renovated Fox Cabaret. Until recently it was a porn theater. Abby points to the new sign. "No more skanky movies. They have live music now." She adds, "Did you know they had to send people in hazmat suits to clean the place out?"

"Gross," I say.

Back at home, Abby retreats to her room and I plunk myself in the rec-room tent. Abby's left a mess—dirty dishes, pens and books, and a huge file folder of vagina-related writing and planning—scattered across the cushions. I sort through the pages, trying to tidy them up. Underneath the papers is the original play by Eve Ensler, a slim book with a pink *V* on the cover. I pick it up warily, then read the introduction, which is about how women don't talk about their vaginas, and Eve Ensler's desire to create a community of women who do. Then I relax into the book. I read the section about the woman who hasn't gone "down there" since 1953, when it betrayed her. I read about rape and giving birth and the letters of the word *cunt*. Then I flip through the monologues Abby and her friends have written: Abby's cunt monologue, the one about suffering through your period, Sunita's "I Am A Sexual Being," the piece by the boy who wants to be a girl, and an anonymous section called "If My Vagina Could Dance"—which I feel responsible for.

If my vagina could dance, it would do a serious tango, all tension and little release. If my vagina could dance, it would be like a Pina Bausch number, all huddled up inside of itself. If my vagina could dance, it would do a kickboxing routine set to Ride of the Valkyries *and destroy menstruation forever.*

*If my vagina could dance…*I don't know how I would finish that sentence.

I scan the monologue titles again. I've heard about most of them from Abby and her friends, except one at the end. It's written by a girl who identifies herself only as C.

Once I had sex and I didn't want to. I guess you'd call it date rape. I left a party with this boy I thought was cute. I didn't know him very well. He was older and had a car. We started driving, and we went somewhere I didn't know, somewhere without a lot of people or houses. He told me he wanted to have sex with me, and I said I didn't want to, but he kept asking and asking and being more demanding and grasping my arms harder and harder. I asked him to take me home, and he said he would, after we did it. And so I let him, because I didn't know where I was and I didn't want to miss my curfew. I didn't want to have to call my parents and try and explain. Also, I didn't want to be bruised. I didn't want to be forced.

I guess you could call it rape. I try not to.

I never told anyone it happened because what difference would it make? And even if it wasn't my fault, I know I shouldn't have gone in the car.

Maybe talking about vaginas is important, so girls will feel empowered, so they won't make stupid mistakes and be flattered by older boys with cars. Maybe if we can talk about our bodies, we'll have power over them. Maybe.

I put the folder down and lie still for a moment. Abby's always going on about bad things happening to girls and women, but I never think about it happening to people at our school, to people we know. I've always thought Abby's play was about her desire to shock people, so she could say *cunt* in public and have people think she was cool. I leave Abby's papers in the tent and wander into the backyard.

I decide to get back on my bike. It's too beautiful an evening to stay inside, and there are so many ideas in my head I can't keep them straight. I head downhill toward the bike path around the inner harbor. I coast past the science center toward Yaletown, cruising by rollerbladers and slow walkers, thinking about C, whoever she is, and her monologue.

All Abby's talk about women and their bodies made Dad give a donation to a women's shelter. And me? The girl in C's monologue could be me, could be any girl. And what am I doing? Nothing. Dad asked me what my passion was. I don't have one yet. The earth needs repairing, and Abby's talking about it all the time, but she's also making change happen. Maybe not earth-shattering change, but change all the same. And me? I'm letting girls like C pile up in my head. A deep chill runs through me.

When I get to English Bay, I get off my bike and sit in the sand against one of the massive logs, with my face up to the sun. A few wispy clouds float across the sky, reminding me of Paul. I almost text him, but I can't think of what to say. I send him a picture of the sky instead. **I'm looking up at the same sky as you**, he writes back. Across the water I can see the sailing club and can almost make out Zeyda's house. I email him, imagining him sitting on his balcony, looking out at the beach where I'm sitting, but he doesn't respond.

The sun sets, and I get back on my bike. The air cools, and I zip my jacket up to my chin. Lights come on as I head back through Yaletown and into Olympic Village, the path emptier now. I shiver as I take in the boats and the city, the night air. I should have dragged Abby with me, made her come out and see the sea and the sunset. She could have danced on the logs the way she used to when we were little. I could have told her I liked some of her monologues.

Abby is not going to be happy until she's onstage with her friends. She needs to find a new venue, some cool little café where they also have folk music or flamenco performances. I'm thinking about this as I start the uphill climb on Main Street. As I pass the Fox Cabaret, I slow down when I see the newly renovated black-and-red facade. Then I get off my bike to look at the list of upcoming events taped to the box-office window. Bands I've never heard of, a drag night, a performance-art show. Would putting on the play here be enough to motivate Abby?

I'm about to get back on my bike when I see a guy going into the building. I hesitate a moment, imagining myself having to talk to a stranger. Then I remember what Dr. Spenser said about reaching out to other people, and I catch up to the guy before the door closes. "Excuse me," I say, "can I ask you about performing here?"

The guy is wearing jeans and a leather jacket and has a shaved head. He's not as old as my parents, but he's not young either. "What kind of performance do you do?" he asks.

I grin, imagining myself performing. "It's not me—it's my sister's play. Our school wouldn't let her do it there."

"No? Why not?"

"Well…" I take a deep breath. "She wanted to do *The Vagina Monologues*, and the school freaked out about the word *cunt*."

The guy rubs his head, looks at me like I might be crazy and then bursts out laughing. "Well, c'mon in, and we'll talk about your sister's play."

An hour later I let myself into our back garden from the lane and find Abby sacked out in the hammock, listening to music on her phone as night falls. I pull up a lawn chair close to her and give her a gentle shove. Abby lifts up her head to look at me and pulls out one earbud. "What?" she asks, looking annoyed.

"About your play," I say.

"The dead one?"

"Yes, that one. I have a surprise for you." I wiggle with excitement.

Abby sighs and lets her head fall back. "Whatever."

"No, listen."

She rolls her eyes and turns to face me. "Fine. What?"

"I went to the Fox Cabaret tonight."

"The where?"

"You know, that place that used to be a porn theater."

"They let you in?"

"Well, it's not like I was there during a show or anything."

Abby's sitting up now. "You went there?"

"Let me finish. It's a beautiful space with a stage and a great sound system now. Way nicer than any school

auditorium." Abby's staring at me, but I keep talking.
"I talked to Mike—"

"Who?"

"Mike—he's the booking manager. Anyway, Mike says you can perform *The Vagina Stories*, or whatever you're calling it, on April 17, which is a Thursday night, or on Saturday the nineteenth. Either day, it has to be at 7:00 PM, because they have a band coming on later. You might want to do it on the Thursday, even if it is a weekday, because this all-girl band called The Tits is playing afterward."

"You're kidding, right?"

I continue, "Now I know you said it wouldn't be good if it wasn't at school, because kids wouldn't see it, so I emailed Mr. Gupta to ask if we could advertise it at school, and I think he'll say yes if the title doesn't have the words *cunt* or *vagina* in it."

"You wrote cunt to Mr. Gupta?"

"Well, no, I said the ad would have school-appropriate language."

"Wait, vagina isn't school-appropriate language?"

"Abby, let's not discuss this now. Mike wants to know if you're in or not, because otherwise they're going to book something else, maybe bingo."

"Are you serious?"

"Yes."

Abby swings her legs out of the hammock and starts pacing the yard. "I don't get it. You're doing this for me?"

"Yes. Oh, I forgot one thing. Mike said that if you want, it can be a fundraiser, and you can take half the house and donate it to a women's cause of your choice."

Abby stops and runs her hands through her hair. "But you hate my play."

"I don't hate your play. I hate the tampon song, and I might insist you cut it if I help you."

"Harsh."

"Oh, and I kinda hate your monologue, but that doesn't mean I don't think it's good."

"Thanks, I think." Abby shakes her head. "Why are you doing this for me?"

I place my hands on my knees and look up at Abby. "Is it so hard to imagine that I might help you? Besides, women's bodies are important."

Abby crinkles her brow. "Since when do you care?"

I shrug. "Are you in?"

Abby sighs. "I'll have to ask the other girls. We really wanted it to be at school."

"I know you did," I say, "and that would have been better. Truly, I think you blew it by including the cunt monologue. But think of this—you're going to perform a version of *The Vagina Monologues* at a place that used to be a porn theater, and instead of it being about the exploitation of women, it's going to be about educating women."

Abby's eyes start to light up. "Ooh," she says. "Take back the theater! I like it! I might have to write a new monologue."

"Shall I text Mike?"

"Not yet. I need to talk to Sunita and the others."

Abby is already up and running into the house before I have time to give her Mike's contact information. I hear her on the phone again and imagine she'll have to write a new song or, worse, a dance. Still, I flop back into my chair, oddly satisfied.

Eleven

THE NEXT MORNING PAUL TEXTS ME. **Mom back to China— want to come over?**

I close my eyes and roll over in bed, tucking my head under my pillow. Can I pretend I haven't seen the text? If I go over and play pool or watch TV, that leather couch in the basement will still be there. Things have been better in the eye-contact part of my life. I've actually had real conversations with Paul about things other than math or investing. I told him some math jokes last week that had him groaning. It felt good, normal.

I text Paul back, **How about the trees?**

The trees?

Remember the ones you sent me the picture of?

Oh right. They won't be in bloom anymore.

That's okay.

Okay then. Let's go see the trees.

I put down my phone and let my head fall back onto my pillow. I'm not brave enough to go to Paul's house, but it should be okay if we meet somewhere in public.

I'm the only one awake, so I make myself some tea, grab a muffin from where Mom's hidden them in the laundry room and take it downstairs. Abby's cleaned up the tent, stacked her books and papers and pens, and taken her dirty dishes upstairs. She's organized her monologues into a folder with a cover page. I scan the table of contents, flip through the pages and find myself reading Sunita's monologue again. *I am a living, breathing creature. I am a sexual being. I am in charge of my own body and all it wants. I live and I breathe and I feel, and I crave too.*

What would that look like? Maybe I could kiss Paul. Maybe I could tell him what I want to do. Whatever that is. I haven't even let my mind go there for the last couple of weeks—it's been too dangerous. Dr. Spenser and I haven't talked about visualizing much lately, but I could try it. I settle myself back on the cushions and close my eyes. Well, I'd like to play with the hair at the back of Paul's neck. And I'd like to kiss him and maybe see what he feels like underneath his shirt. I'm curious about his skin, what it would feel like next to mine, how smooth it might be and what it would taste like under his ear. I spend a few more minutes thinking about Paul, not only his smile and the way he scratches his head with his pencil or twists his eyebrows together when he's working on a math problem, but also the way he smiles at me and makes me want to smile back. *Let me tell you what I want,* Sunita wrote. I feel my pulse pick up. Usually I back away at this point. What if I didn't? What if I let myself give in to those feelings? What if I followed Dr. Spenser's suggestion and took a risk? I could have a new metaphor. What if instead of *if you touch me I'll break in two,* it could be *if I kiss you we'll be a fire, but not the kind that burns down houses*? I like this image. I take out my journal and start writing.

> *If I kiss you we'll create a fire,*
> *not one that burns down houses*
> *but that lights up a city*
> *or makes northern lights flare across the sky*
>
> *If I kiss you we'll be a raging storm,*
> *not one that ruins farmers' fields*
> *but one that makes rivers flow in dried-up beds*
> *or creeks gurgle with rainbow-fleshed fish*
>
> *If I kiss you we'll make a small quiet space,*
> *not one with broken pieces and fear*
> *but one that glows with a private light*
> *where we speak a language only we understand*

I look at the words on the page, reread them and make a few small changes. I'm not trying to work language down to the smallest bits I can find. Instead I'm building something, creating something bigger than me, maybe bigger than Paul and me. I think I might have written something I like. I sit still, listening to the beat of my heart, feeling the exhilaration of not wanting to rip the pages out of my book. Part of me wants to spin around the room, but I don't want to break the spell of having written a poem that captures how I feel. And what if there's more in me?

I flip through my journal, looking for lines I like, copying them on a fresh page of my journal in my neatest printing. Most of what I've written is awful, but I find a few lines I like. I pause when I come to the "I Fear" free-write. I haven't looked at it since I wrote it. I could never bring myself to actually throw it out—it felt like it contained everything that was important to me, everything that mattered. I was the sum of my fears.

Now I take a deep breath and write each fear at the top of a separate page, *I fear tsunamis, I fear Zeyda going crazy, I fear crashing on my bike*, and then, on the last page, *I fear not being able to get up in the morning.* I do a free-write on each of these, my writing becoming tiny and illegible at the bottom of the pages and sneaking around the sides, even leaking around to the back. I have to cross out some of the titles and rewrite them. My writing gets slanted and fills with indecipherable loops and weird shorthand I didn't know I knew. *I fear Zeyda's house filling with water, the wave splashing high into his living room, and then leaking down through the rest of the house, Chinese vases and carved tables floating and bobbing out broken windows into the cold sea. Zeyda and Crystal float on a raft made from the lid of the grand piano my mother played as a child.* By the time I get to the last fear, about not being able to get out of bed in the morning, my pen moves so quickly I'm jotting down half ideas, words bleeding into each other to get them all down. *I fear not being able to get up in the morning but it already happened, and it was awful, Abby's sad face, forgetting to worry about everyone else, and heaviness, but a way out, a way out, although it's not totally gone, what if the meds don't work, what if, what if, what if? It will happen again and there will be people to help me, right? 'Cause I'm not alone. My mother, not her, but her, she will pry me out. Lock the closet if she has to. My mother, and Fenny savior Penny and Paul, waiting for me, Paul waiting for me.*

I've been ignoring my phone for so long that when Paul calls it wrenches me from where I've been—lost in words, somewhere deep inside my head. I jump and clutch at the phone, my hello sounding shell-shocked.

"Hey," he says, "you okay?"

I swallow, gripping my journal to stabilize myself. "Yes."

"Did you forget about hanging out today?"

"Oh. No."

"Did I wake you?"

"No," I say. "I was concentrating." I want to put the phone down and go back to my journal. "Can I call you later?" I know I sound impatient.

"Okay," Paul says, sounding uncertain. "Is everything okay?"

"Yes, fine. I'm in the middle of something. I'll call you in an hour." I hang up as Paul is saying goodbye and go back to my writing. Each of my fears slowly becomes a poem, the catalog of my worries and anxieties, like exhaling a long breath, like getting the worry out of my head and onto my paper. I write a few more pages, each one with a topic for a poem scrawled at the top: *Dr. Spenser, Abby's play, Fen.* Finally I come to Paul. I struggle to write what I want, about being on the leather couch, the feelings sliding up my legs, what Sunita wrote in her monologue. I want to be with Paul, and I want to let myself experience all the feelings that I usually squash down.

I write until I am so wrung out I can only lie on the floor and stare at the ceiling. Paul is texting me and I'm hungry for lunch and I don't want to move, not because of the fog, but because I've kicked some of the thoughts out of my head and onto paper, and some of it is good. Some of it might be good enough to send to Paul, to read to Sofia, to hand in for my assignment. It makes me want to dance through the house, spinning. I've captured the thoughts buzzing in my restless mind, and now they're like butterflies soaring with their wings spread wide. The words are beautiful, and they're mine.

When I meet Paul to bike to VanDusen Garden, I'm so excited I almost forget to be nervous. The easy, graceful way he rides his bicycle, all relaxed limbs and a casual wave when he sees me, makes me even happier. It's a beautiful, warm day, breezy, with the smell of lilacs drifting by us as we bike toward Oak Street. We lock our bikes at the park entrance, pay the entrance fee and stroll down a gravel path past a vegetable garden and some bushes carved into animal shapes. Paul leads us along a path lined with flowers and then by a pond with ducks. I let him hold my hand even though it makes me feel a little queasy.

"Your mom left for China?" I say.

Paul swings my hand. "Yep. But she's going to come back for the whole summer."

Paul looks happy, so I say, "That's good. How was your visit?"

"Mostly okay. We went to the outlet mall near Seattle. She cooked a lot. We talked about school too." Paul sighs. "She's going to ask my dad about me doing a double major—biology and economics."

"She's okay with that?"

"Not really, but she doesn't want me to be miserable either."

"What about your dad?"

Paul grins. "Oh, he's probably okay with me being miserable. You're lucky your parents are so normal."

I shrug. "I think they just want me to be okay."

Paul stops walking and looks at me. "And are you okay?"

I take a deep breath. I didn't feel the fog when I woke up this morning. Maybe it's because of biking yesterday, or maybe the meds are starting to work. "I think I'm starting to feel better."

"That's cool." Paul's grinning now and tugging gently on my hand. "Look." He points across a lawn. "There are the trees." Farther down the path a small grove of cherry trees shimmers in the light, each one with a canopy of green leaves. We walk toward them and look up at the branches. "You could take pictures of them in different seasons," I say. "Like a series."

"Maybe." Paul walks around the grove and holds up his phone to take a picture. "There's a mycology group that meets here monthly to look at mushrooms. I'm thinking of joining, except I think it might be only old people."

"Maybe some young cute girls are also interested in mushrooms," I say.

"Maybe. I don't think I'm interested in other girls." He looks like he's going to walk over and kiss me, and I start to feel my usual panic rise. I think about Sunita's monologue.

"Do you want to sit under the trees?" I blurt out.

"Sure." Paul sits down in the grass, his arms around his knees, and looks up at me as if to say, *Are you coming?* "I want to take a picture of you," I say to buy myself time. Paul smiles at me, and I pull out my phone and snap a photo of him under the green boughs, and then another and another, until I feel ridiculous. I slowly kneel beside him. He leans back and looks up at the branches, up at me. He squeezes my foot and leans toward me. I can tell he's going to kiss me, so before he does, I kiss him quickly on the cheek. "Don't move," I whisper. "Okay?"

Paul nods. When I don't do anything for a moment, he looks at me expectantly. I take a deep breath and lean over and sniff his skin. I close my eyes and lean my face on his shoulder. Then I let my lips brush against his neck. He sits very still, letting me lean into him. I rest my hands on his shoulders, feeling the muscles underneath. Paul has a quizzical look on his face, as if he's not sure what's going to happen next, but there's a hint of a smile on his lips too.

"You look relaxed," I say.

Paul closes his eyes. "I'm always relaxed with you."

"How come?"

"I don't know. It feels right."

This makes me smile, makes me feel brave. "I'm going to kiss you," I say into his ear.

"I won't stop you."

And so I kiss his ear first, the full lobe and then the outer shell of it. I can hear his breathing pick up as I leave small kisses across his cheek to his lips. I think about my poem. I can do this, even as Paul's hands come up and rest on the small of my back. My lips find his and we're kissing, and I want to be here, under this tree with Paul, with my arms coming up to wrap around him. I am holding Paul. I can do this.

We leave a few hours later, our clothes mussed, lips swollen from kisses, my hair full of grass that Paul patiently picks out for me before we bike home. We kiss for a long time in the back lane behind my house before I finally say goodbye and slip into the yard. I skip past Abby listening to music in the hammock and throw myself into the tent. Sofia wants to know how my date with Paul was. I text her, **It was good.** I add, **I was brave.**

She texts me back a happy face, and I wrap my arms around myself. Paul and I are going to see each other later tonight maybe, and then at school tomorrow, and then maybe every day after that. And I won't be nervous, because it's Paul.

Abby's play is still in the tent, and I pick it up and riffle through the pages again, rereading "If My Vagina Could Dance." Once I told Abby that my vagina doesn't dance. And now? Maybe it does, a little bit. I pick up one of Abby's pencils and write on a sticky note. *If my vagina could dance, it would…well, it would be really shy. And private. And maybe it wouldn't exactly dance, maybe it would swoon a little bit. But I wouldn't tell anyone about it.* I attach the sticky note to one of the last pages of the play and look at it there, in my handwriting, in Abby's play. I decide this is where it should stay.

Then I flip through my journal and reread the vagina monologue Sofia convinced me to write. I sit thinking about it for a few minutes and make some changes, adding a few ideas and cutting out extra words. I decide to call it "The Most Dangerous Thing." Then I type it into my phone and send it to Sofia. She texts me back, **I LOVE this. You are brave!** I sit looking at this text for a few minutes, feeling proud of myself. Then I take a deep breath and copy the monologue onto a blank piece of paper. I slip it into Abby's manuscript pages. For a moment I feel sick to my stomach and almost rip it out, but that feeling passes, and I carefully put Abby's play back in the tent.

Twelve

PAUL AND I LIE UNDER THE BIG WILLOW TREE at the back of the field behind the school during lunch hour. For the first time I don't feel on edge with him. When Paul wraps his arms around me and I breathe in the scent of his neck, it makes my head feel so clear I want to sigh. The sky over Paul's shoulder is a bright blue, with the kind of fluffy clouds that make me think of angels. When the bell rings for class, Paul presses his face into my hair, and shivers run down my spine.

"What are you doing after school?" he asks as we get up to walk across the field. We hold hands, swinging our arms.

"I have to go see my zeyda today, and then I'm busy tomorrow too. It's a Jewish holiday."

"Oh yeah? What kind of holiday?"

I tell Paul a little about Passover, that it's a celebration of freedom from slavery. He listens intently and asks what we eat and if we have to wear special clothes, and I end up giving him a lot of details about the Seder. "That sounds interesting," he says.

"I guess it is," I say. "Today I have to convince my grandfather to come. He thinks we're heathens because my mom is changing some of the traditions."

Paul sighs. "I know all about family members being reluctant to change."

After school I walk all the way to Paul's with him so we can kiss on his front doorstep. Then I bike to Zeyda's and plunk myself onto a chair across from him on his back deck. The downtown buildings shimmer in the sunlight; the harbor is full of sailboats and kayaks. The tide is out, and I can see people walking in the wet sand along the beach. Zeyda is slumped in his chair, wearing a sun hat and the kind of old-man sunglasses that completely cover his regular glasses.

"You're extra late today." Zeyda straightens himself up, and I can tell he's glad to see me.

"I was with Paul," I say.

"He must be your boyfriend."

I grin and duck my head. "Maybe you'll even meet him one day."

Zeyda rolls his eyes. "How about a game of checkers?"

I shake my head. "I can't stay too long, because I promised Mom I would help her cook for the Seder."

"Oh, right. Passover is tomorrow." Zeyda's face falls into its usual grumpy lines. "What are you making?"

"Tonight I'm making matzah balls, and tomorrow, probably a salad. Oh, and tsimmes."

"Sounds delicious."

"Well, if you came, you could try my new tsimmes recipe."

Zeyda crosses his arms, his face deepening into a scowl. "I'm planning my own Seder."

"Oh, who's coming?" I ask.

"Well, maybe you and Crystal." Zeyda's eyebrows rise hopefully.

I bite my lip and then take a deep breath. "Zeyda, that sounds really sad. Besides, Crystal and I can't come, so come to Mom's, okay?"

Zeyda flaps a hand in the air. "Bah. I'll stay home and drink four Scotches by myself instead of four cups of wine."

I flop back in my chair. "Remind me why you're so opposed to Mom's Seder?"

Zeyda grips the arms of his chair, his knuckles white. "Your mother changes the words from the way the prayers are written. She adds things that aren't supposed to be there."

"But Zeyda, the only commandment for Passover is to tell the story. I know it's important to eat the special Passover foods, but it doesn't say anywhere you can't add things. Doesn't religion have to change to keep up with the times?"

"Is tradition such a bad thing?" Zeyda asks.

"Is it such a good thing?" I try a different tactic. "Why don't you ask Mom if you can lead some parts of the Seder? What's the most important part?"

Zeyda thinks for a minute. "The blessings."

"Then ask Mom if you can do them. You can lead them any way you want. Mom will add extra stuff, but you can do your part."

Zeyda thinks about this. "You mean compromise?"

"Yeah."

"I've never been so good at that."

I tap Zeyda's knee. "Well, maybe it's time."

"There's an expression about old dogs and new tricks."

"What's this really about?"

Zeyda looks away from me. I don't say anything, just let the silence well up between us. Finally Zeyda says, "Your bubbie made the best Passover dessert, this thing with Cool Whip and meringues and coffee. I don't know how she did it."

"I remember that. I think Abby's making it for dessert this year."

"Your bubbie also made such good gefilte fish, from scratch, and matzah balls and delicious chicken soup and macaroons. Her turkey was very tender."

I listen to Zeyda list all the Passover foods Bubbie once made, and watch the sadness funnel up through him.

When he finishes speaking, I sit for a moment, remembering all the Seders we used to have at Bubbie and Zeyda's house, how much fun Bubbie always made the Seder for the kids. I get up and wrap my arms tight around Zeyda, tight enough that I hear him groan a little. I whisper in his ear, "We're going to eat all those foods. Dad and Mom and their friends and me and Abby—we're making it. All of it, the fish and the soup and even the gross macaroons." I squeeze Zeyda a little tighter. "Dad and I are coming to pick you and Crystal up at 5:00 PM, okay?"

For a moment I think Zeyda is going to wrestle out of my arms. Then I feel him relax, a kind of melting defeat. He nods and slumps his shoulders. I kiss his forehead and wipe away the tear that has edged down his cheek.

After dinner I'm making a cup of tea in the kitchen when Abby corners me, her manuscript in hand. She's been her normal self, singing and dancing and planning, since she agreed to put on the play at the Fox.

"I see," she says, her eyebrows arched, "that you've been tampering with my masterpiece."

I focus on adding sugar to my tea. "No," I say.

"Then what's this?" She fans through the papers to show me the sticky note and monologue I added.

"I have no idea." I turn to put the box of tea back in the cupboard, but I can feel Abby staring at me.

"It's in your handwriting," she says.

I glance over at the pages. "No it's not."

"Syd, I know your handwriting."

"Fine. If you don't want it, I'll take it right back." I reach toward the manuscript, but Abby pulls it away.

"Leave it." She smiles coyly. "Does this mean you want to perform?"

"Oh god, no. I could never say those words in public."

Abby hugs her play to her chest. "You definitely have issues."

"I'm working on them," I say quietly, sipping my tea.

"You should. Paul will appreciate it."

I elbow her in the side. Abby holds her ribs and steps away. "You know, I used to think you were really shallow," she says, helping herself to some nuts from a jar on the counter.

"Thanks."

"Now I think there's more to you."

"That's great," I say. "My whole life is more meaningful now that it has your seal of approval."

Abby cocks her head to the side. "Maybe you could do a voice-over."

"What do you mean?"

"We could record you reading your monologue and play it during the performance. Sunita and I made a slide show that needs music or text. It might work."

"So I wouldn't really be performing, but my words would be in the show?"

"Right."

Neither of us says anything for a moment. Then I blurt out, "Sofia wrote a monologue too. You might like it."

"What's it about?"

"It's about…girl parts, and you know…" I struggle to find the right word. "Sex," I finally say.

Abby grins. "Sounds interesting. We're rehearsing in about an hour. Tell her to come." She saunters out of the kitchen.

I sit on the floor with my tea cradled in my hands. Then I pick up my phone. I type Sofia a message. **Vagina monologue rehearsal tonight. A says you can come.**

Sofia types back, **For real?**

I hesitate. **Yes.**

I'm in if you are.

I take a long time responding. Finally I type, **Okay.**

An hour later I'm in the basement with Abby, Sunita, Sofia and some of the other members from the cast. Sofia is nervous and pacing around the room, the high heels she's chosen to wear clicking on the linoleum. I hover by the door. When Abby invites her to read her piece, Sofia flips her hair around and changes her stance a few times before beginning. She speaks her opening line, *"Every girl has a button,"* with uncertainty, her voice wavering, but then gets louder, more sure of herself. She giggles nervously at the end when the other girls clap.

"Wow," Abby says. "That was powerful."

The other girls nod and start discussing the best place to add Sofia's monologue. When Sofia sits down with the others, she beckons for me to join her. I perch on the edge of a cushion next to her. She wraps one arm around me and gives me a squeeze. I can feel her hands shaking. "Thanks," she says, and I'm not sure for what exactly, but I also understand.

"I think I found some text for the slide show Sunita and I made," Abby announces. "It's a short but really powerful piece. The author wants to be anonymous." I bury my face in Sofia's shoulder as Abby reads my title. "*The Most Dangerous Thing.*" Then she projects the slide show against the rec-room wall. I'd imagined embarrassing images of vaginas, but the pictures are of girls, all different girls, tall and short, beautiful and not, from different ethnic backgrounds. This is even more difficult to look at, as if I'm imagining all those girls and their dangerous desires, their anxieties and needs. Abby reads slowly, ending with my final question. "*What if we talked about the dangers of sex for girls, but also the bliss?*"

Everyone remains silent for a moment, watching the final images. Then Sunita says, "I think we should end with this. I think it sends a really positive message."

Abby nods. "It would be nice to end on a happy note."

Sofia squeezes my hand tightly, and I squeeze back.

"Who will read it?" one of the girls asks.

"The girl who wrote it might record herself," Abby says. "She's thinking about it."

The other girls start talking about the lighting for the show and what music to play while people are entering the cabaret. I stand up and motion for Sofia to follow me. I run up the stairs, pulling her behind me, and then out the front door and onto the sidewalk. The night is clear and cool, with a brilliant sky. I feel like running down the street to release all the energy inside me, but Sofia grabs me by the shoulders and pulls me to her in a tight hug. She whispers in my hair, "You're no chicken."

Then we run down the street toward her condo, holding hands, not stopping until we have to wait for the traffic light at Main Street.

The next day I have permission to skip Mandarin to come home early for Passover. The turkey is in the oven, the soup and matzah balls ready to be reheated. The dining-room table has been extended to its maximum length, with two extra card tables added to the end of it, sticking out into the living room past the couch. Abby's cutting vegetables in the kitchen while Dad makes the kugel. I help Mom set the table, putting out the plates and napkins while she arranges place cards based on her seating plan.

"Zeyda called to announce he's doing the blessings," Mom says.

I put down the stack of napkins. "I told him to ask or suggest, to make a compromise."

"Well, that's not what it sounded like."

"I hope you said yes."

"Of course. I said, What a great idea."

"So he's coming?"

"It seems so."

Paul texts me a picture of a monarch butterfly. He writes, **Do you know caterpillars liquefy before they become butterflies in the chrysalis?**

Gross, I text back.

Where r u?

I had to leave early to get ready for Passover.

Oh, right.

I can hear Paul's loneliness even in his text. "Hey, Mom, how many people are coming tonight?"

"Seventeen including Zeyda."

"Do you think you have room for one more?"

"Probably. Miri's son canceled."

"Do you think I could invite Paul?"

Mom puts down the Haggadahs and looks at me, surprised.

"I think he's alone a lot, and it might be nice for him to be around people."

Mom presses her lips together. "But Syd, he's probably never been to a Jewish dinner of any kind. Won't he feel awkward?"

"Maybe, but I told him about it, and he said it sounded interesting."

Mom hesitates a moment. "It would be better if he came another night."

"Oh. Is Sunita coming?"

"Yes, but she's been here for Shabbat before, right? But it's up to you. If you think he won't feel uncomfortable, then invite him."

"I'll ask him if he wants to come."

Mom reorganizes the place cards to make a place for Paul next to me. Then she starts organizing musical instruments—shakers and drums in a basket, her guitar on its stand by the end of the table.

I text Paul. **Our dinner tonight will be weird and long, but you're welcome to come.**

A few minutes later Paul writes, **Thinking about it.** I go back to setting the table. Then he writes, **Would I have to wear a beanie?**

I smile. He means a *kippah.* I type, **Beanie would be optional, I think.**

Then I'm in.

Okay, come at 5:30.

I'm nervous about exposing Paul to a whole family Seder, and who knows what Mom's got planned exactly. I feel extra nervous when she starts sprinkling little finger puppets around the table. "What are those?" I ask.

"They're plague puppets."

"What?"

She picks up a red puppet in the shape of a drop of blood. "See, this is the blood plague." She means the first plague, when the rivers turned to blood. I notice the other puppets are wild beasts, hail, locusts and even lice. There are ten in all, one for each of the plagues in the Passover story.

"That's gross and disgusting," I say.

"At least dinner won't be boring," she says.

I pick up my phone and write to Paul. **FYI, my mom is really crazy, and dinner is going to be like performance theater with at least an hour of ritual before we eat. Are you sure you still want to come?**

I'm in, Paul writes back. **Should I bring anything?**

An empty stomach and lots of tolerance. And a sense of humor.

"Syd, put the phone down, please."

Gotta go, I type. **Dress like you're coming to a party.**

No hoodie?

No hoodie.

Mom and I finish setting the table, and then I make the tsimmes while she works on the Seder plate. Abby washes the lettuce and cuts the carrots for the gefilte fish. By the time we're done, there is just enough time to change for dinner and help Dad get Zeyda's wheelchair up the front stairs of the house.

Soon after we get Zeyda inside, Miri and Todd arrive with their daughter, Rachel, and her husband, then the

Levs and Auntie Karen and Uncle Mark and Sunita too. The house fills with happy voices, everyone carrying food into the kitchen and wishing each other a Happy Passover. Paul is the last person to arrive. He's wearing a white shirt with a tie and dark pants; his hair is gelled up. He has brought flowers and gives them to Mom for the table. "See?" I say to Zeyda as we watch Paul talking to Mom. "You said a nice boy brings flowers." I point to the bouquet of tulips Crystal is putting in a vase.

Zeyda says, "I didn't know he was coming."

"It was a last-minute thing. He was kinda like you."

Zeyda raises both his eyebrows.

"Lonely and he didn't have a Seder to go to."

Zeyda scowls.

"Oh, c'mon. Tonight is supposed to be about freedom from slavery. Try and be happy."

Zeyda only glowers in response.

Mom and Dad start asking people to find their place cards and sit down at the table. I wheel Zeyda to his place between Mom and me and watch Paul walk toward me.

"Your dad gave me a beanie to wear," Paul says, pointing to the silver kippah resting on top of his spiky hair.

I laugh a little. "It looks okay." Then I tap Zeyda's shoulder. "Zeyda, this is Paul."

Paul says, "Nice to meet you," and shakes Zeyda's hand across me. I look around the table, feeling a little self-conscious sitting next to Paul. Then Mom raises

her voice. "Welcome, everyone, and Happy Passover."
There is a chorus of Happy Passover greetings. She smiles.
"We'll begin our Seder on page six of the Haggadah."

"This first song tells the order of all the things we're
going to do tonight," I whisper to Paul. I've always liked
that there's a checklist of items.

"There's a lot of them," Paul whispers, looking at
his page.

"Yep."

And then Mom leads us all in the opening song, her
voice strong and clear. The rest of us join in—Auntie
Karen and Uncle Mark, the Levs, even Dad and Zeyda,
with his croaky, unused voice, and finally me. Paul shifts
in his chair, a little uncomfortable but smiling anyway.
My feet tap nervously under the table as I imagine how
strange Paul must think this, all of us singing together
around a table. Then I wonder what everyone else thinks
of Paul being here, if they're saying things about him
being my boyfriend. I try to focus on the words on the
page to fight the heat climbing my cheeks.

At some point in the Seder Mom is going to ask
everyone what freedom means to them. Most people will
say they're thankful for living in a place like Canada, or
for their good health and families. I think about all the
things I might say: that freedom is being able to get out of
bed, or to see clearly; that freedom is to feel the tremble of
nervous excitement I do now rather than the fog. I can't
say this in front of everyone, and even thinking about

it makes me want to get up from the table, to make an excuse to check something in the kitchen. I can't abandon Paul, so I take a deep breath and squeeze his hand under the table. He squeezes back and whispers in my ear, "There is food at the end of this, right?"

"Yes, lots," I say.

Paul grins. "Good. I'm starving."

Abby looks across the table at Paul and me and gives me a thumbs-up. Part of me wants to hide under my bangs, but I'm also happy. Maybe this is freedom too—being with Paul in front of everyone, letting him be part of my family and all its craziness. I haven't told Paul about the monologues yet. No doubt I'll feel like barfing while I tell him, and I'll want to run away screaming if he asks if he can come. And yet, even as I squirm in my seat, I know I'm going to record my monologue, and that Paul will come and recognize my voice in the play, hear my words. Maybe I'll send him my monologue before that. Maybe I'll even send it to Dr. Spenser. I take a deep breath and try to digest all these thoughts. I squeeze Paul's hand a little too intensely, and he looks at me quizzically. I smile back at him and loosen my grip on his hand. Yes, I think, these are all small steps toward freedom.

Acknowledgments

Many thanks to Jen Davidson-Harden and Nancy Salay for their friendship and helpful discussions; to Marcy Lieberman, Sharon Meehan and Elsie Sze for their suggestions on drafts of this novel; and to Sarah Harvey for her guidance and careful editing. Inga Musico's *Cunt: A Declaration of Independence*, Peggy Orenstein's *Girls and Sex: Navigating the Complicated New Landscape* and Eve Ensler's *The Vagina Monologues* were all indispensable to my writing. I am also grateful to the Ontario Arts Council for supporting this project.

LEANNE LIEBERMAN is a the author of four acclaimed YA novels, including *Gravity* (a Sydney Taylor Notable book) and *Lauren Yanofsky Hates the Holocaust*. Her adult fiction has been published in *Descant, Grain, The New Quarterly, The Antigonish Review* and other magazines. Leanne lives with her family in Kingston, Ontario, where she teaches elementary school (including sex ed).

More great reads by
LEANNE LIEBERMAN

"Lauren's narration is contemplative and from the heart, and readers should relate to her attempts to identify her beliefs and tackle life's big questions."

—*Publishers Weekly*

9781459801097 pb $12.95

Leanne Lieberman

Gravity

9781554690497 pb $12.95

"A remarkably sensitive and credible portrait of a girl whose faith collides with her sexuality, and who refuses to compromise either."
—*The Bulletin of the Center for Children's Books*

"[A] realistic, sensitively drawn story of one teen's tumultuous, coming-of-age search for faith, cultural identity, and grown-up love."
—*Booklist*

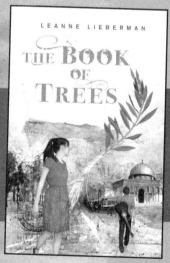

LEANNE LIEBERMAN

THE BOOK OF TREES

9781554692651 pb $12.95